(continued from inside front cover)

"The voices from *The Digital Ho* r—often painful, never predictable. Whet u by the throat and won't let go until they'

—JILL NELSO *Chaser*

"P.J.'s work hits like a brick. The rea st quick dips into e spray-painted on a wall. P.J. wraps Chicano, Puerto Rican, black, every shade of Latino and Anglo city life, hooks L.A. and New York, South Bronx, and Newark and layers it all together like a skilled burrito maker."

—ABRAHAM RODRIGUEZ, Jr., author of *Spidertown*

P. J. RONDINONE grew up in the South Bronx. His stories have appeared in *Mississippi Review*, *Fiction International*, *Another Chicago Review*, *African Voices*, and elsewhere. He is an English professor and director of journalism at a CUNY community college and lives in New York. His Web site is www.peterrondinone.simplenet.com.

JACKET DESIGN: HENRY SENE YEE
CD BOOKLET PHOTOGRAPH: JOSEPH RODRIGUEZ/BLACK STAR
CD JEWEL CASE PHOTOGRAPH: BARRY MARCUS
AUTHOR PHOTOGRAPH: SUSAN DABOLL

Picador USA

A DIVISION OF ST. MARTIN'S PRESS · 175 FIFTH AVENUE, NEW YORK, N.Y. 10010
Distributed by McClelland & Stewart Inc. in Canada · Printed in the U.S.A.

The Digital Hood

The Digital Hood

and Other Stories

P. J. RONDINONE

Picador USA
New York

Grateful acknowledgment is made to the following publications in which these stories first appeared: *Black Water Review* and *Private Arts*, "Something for Sucio"; *Mississippi Review*, "The Nobody" and "Faux Pas"; *Rosebud*, "Cleopatra"; *River Styx*, "Gangsta Bond"; *RE Arts & Letters*, " The Male Bond"; *Another Chicago Magazine*, "Miss Mandi and Me"; *Struggle*, "Glasses"; *Uno Mas*, "You People"; *Fiction International*, "To Break a Nigga's Neck"; *Spike*, "Zap-a-Ho"; *Wascana Review*, "The Tooth Fairy"; *African Voices*, "The Digital Hood."

DESIGN BY MAUREEN TROY

Library of Congress Cataloging-in-Publication Data

Rondinone, P. J.
The digital hood : stories / P. J. Rondinone. — 1st ed.
p. cm.
ISBN 0-312-18686-X
I. Title.
PS3568.0568D5 1998
813'.54—dc21 98-5377
CIP

First Picador USA Edition: July 1998
10 9 8 7 6 5 4 3 2 1

To Professor Richard Goldstone,
Professor Ross Alexander,
Professor Frederic Tuten,
Francine duPlessix Gray,
Donald Barthelme,
Frederick Barthelme,
Susan Sontag,
Michael Oreskes,
E. J. Dionne Jr.,
my agent, Elizabeth Backman,
my editor, George Witte,
my mom, my brothers,
my sister Debbie, Errol Selkirk,
my old Davidson Boy *Louis Alicea,*
and finally to my best readers—
my wife, Kathrine Jason,
and my daughter, Micole.

Contents

The Digital Hood

Something for Sucio

There's something Sucio gotta know, being a home slice 'n' all, being he's fucked up 'n' shit—and we can't have fuck-ups in the hood. We're like, putting a bullet in his head, knowing he'd be down with it—like *whassup*?

But we can't figure who's tellin' the sucker, though we know he's gonna like this part—the last supper, the beef, which is the *thing* that got us stuck, hear what I'm saying?

But like, *how big a nut ought the nigga get?* These days, it ain't easy getting paid.

Froggy (Sucio's main man) says that Sucio is stupid fresh for rice pudding and Cherry Cokes. "He eats the shit every day, yo." And that's def with us 'n' all, but Sucio's bitch Pookie gets in everybody's face.

She says, "If Sucio is goin' down with us, if he's puttin' a bullet in his head for us 'n' shit, we could *at least* show the fucker some respect. Rice pudding ain't nothing to catch a bullet."

And I'm down with that. I tell the niggers to step off and turn out their pockets. And they know I don't profile. I'm not square to the wood. But no one got jack to spend on Sucio. So Pookie says, "Fuck it. I'll make my okra chicken."

But then, yo, my man Zoom-O says that Pookie's got paint chipping off her kitchen walls 'n' shit and we don't want no one catching the lead poisoning, 'cept Sucio, who's getting it in the head. He says, "We gotta give the nigger a party—*at least*!"

Now, everybody knows that Sucio is one partying mamma jamma. And Zoom-O says he'll let us use his apartment. But I wonder, Like yo? What about the pit bull, Zoom-O? Everybody *knows* what Sucio did to Tommy Lee's dog.

We was sleeping in Tommy's basement. Then Pookie woke up and saw Sucio with his dick out, his mushroom in that dog's mouth 'n' all. And we all laughed 'n' shit. But yo, the louder we got the more he slapped that dick into the dog's face. And when we couldn't stand it any longer—*yo*, we was laughing so hard—Sucio screamed: "Meeees-ter, I'm coming, meeester!"

That's why we named the raspberry *Sucio*, which means dirty in Puerto Rican.

But if this is going to be a real party, I got to thinking: What about the invitations? What they gonna say? I realized . . . like making these up ain't easy.

Then Pookie put it straight up. "Ain't no one coming to a good-bye unless there's some fly music and drugs 'n' shit." Which is when my man Zoom-O said, "Then fuck it. I'll put my bull on the roof. We can use my crib but ain't no way I'm letting you niggers blow Sucio's nasty brains up on my walls. Not at my place, yo."

And that's why I'm president. BTS, my crew, Born to Stomp, depend on me 'n' all to figure things out. I first got the idea to run it down to Sucio: Why we can't have fucking up no more. But I had backup, hear what I'm saying? My gat, my cronz, was close to my heart and if he jumped salty, I'd burn his ass twice real fast. And I know, if one day some rapper sings a song about my life he's gonna say:

Since I was a youth
I smoked weed out
Now I'm that
That you read about

Taking a life or two
If I got to
That's what the hell I do.

And Sucio knows this shit foe-one-foe. Which is why he was cool with me and said if he had to, he was doing himself. And I respected that, and I promised he could pick his own gat 'n' shit, any gun he wanted—two gats, pick *one.*

Pookie even set it up with her woman Mermaid, who took out a bag and spread the shit on Tommy's table. Mermaid smiled and said, "Death for sale, motherfuckers." And I realized I liked the bitch and maybe one day we could go out and see a movie 'n' shit. Maybe we could bump the uglies, yo. But that was later. Mermaid had a dope selection:

-a Colt .45 Peacemaker
-a Glock Model 23, .40 caliber
-an HK4 firing .22, .32, or .380 caliber by changing the barrel
-a Smith & Wesson .357 Magnum Revolver
-a Roughrider .22 caliber
-a Colt Trooper Mak III .357
-a Glock 19

"Take your pick," said Mermaid, still sweet tooth 'n' shit.

Pookie was the first, and the fastest. She said Sucio had a dick *thang* for racing cars, watching demolition derbies 'n' shit; he liked them engines exploding in barrels of smoke, the drivers pulled from their wrecks, helmets burning 'n' shit. She said the Trooper Mak III sounded like them Mach speeds Sucio was always yapping about, saying he was getting a jeep and fixing it up 'n' shit once he got enough G to set Mr. T bumping. But everybody knew the only thing this nigger was driving was on a video screen for twenty-five cents.

But Froggy said he didn't play it like that. He figured Sucio for an HK4. That way his main man could choose the caliber going into his head—the size of the lead. If Sucio felt bad, he could go heavy with the changing barrel, yo, the .380. But if he was running with the juice, he might go E-light with the .22 caliber.

But then, yo, my man Zoom-O was quick to let us know: Buying lead cost money 'n' all. We don't want to spend more than we got to. We got drugs and music to lay out. So I said I'd talk to Sucio about it, knowing that before he fucked up he was always down with the posse. He knows that getting paid, these days, ain't that easy.

Like the time Froggy herbed that ol' humpback. That bitch put a cane stitch to his skull. He had a forty-ounce, and I don't mean malt liquor. And he only got twenty bucks; twenty bucks and we had to lock down in Tommy's basement for a whole fucking week, hiding from the cops 'n' shit, with that dog jumping for everybody's dick—*yo.*

If we need money to party, yo, then we gotta hit them megabucks! Pookie's right—we gotta hit some drug-dealing motherfuckers. But we gotta do it far away, like in Queens, and we gotta bone 'em good and dry. And if we do it right, Froggy says, we can even get those invitations made in a copy shop, on shiny red paper 'n' shit.

But still, we gotta settle this thing big time with Sucio. He gotta pick his gun and he gotta decide: Does he want a blindfold, his chest to a wall, his heart beating against the brick? Does he want a knit cap and a cap in his neck, down on his knees? Does he want a chair and a pop between the eyes? Does he want to lie down, a pillow for his feet? Or does he want what I think is best?

We'll dig a hole in the Bronx Park, overlooking the waterfalls. That way, a cap to the head and he goes ka-plunk, his ass falls straight into the grave. *Totally yes!*

Pookie says the park is good. Since it will be June, the trees will be green and leafy 'n' shit. That'll give the whole thing a nice, natural feeling.

But what if it rains? Zoom-O got the jump on me. I was thinking the same thing. Then everybody will be pissed and the food will go bad!

But Froggy wanted to know, "What if Sucio, the last minute, decides that he wants like a firing squad? That would be just like his ass, to let his ego take over, imagining himself with a cigarette dangling from his lips, blowing smoke rings at us while we line up, raise up, and shoot on the count of three."

But there's no way. I remind everybody that Sucio already knows that he's in deep shit for his fucking up 'n' all, and I told him we won't have fucking up. No more.

He always wore two gold rings on every finger, bragging that every finger was a virgin he popped. He bragged that he did the seven-year-olds, slapping their titties left and right, real gangstalike, making them suck his dick 'n' shit, like Tommy's dog. And that's fucked up 24/7. We all agreed on that.

Pookie didn't even know it. She knew he was a sick bastard, and she laughed. Like when he got drunk and puked his guts out, he always said he never washed his mouth until he kissed a girl. He said bitches liked that shit. He said it made them hot in the twat!

But fucking with a seven-year-old? We all figured that pussy got to be ripe (at least thirteen) before it got to be boned. Even Pookie didn't give it up until she was fourteen.

That's when the shooter came up. Who is pulling the trigger? I grew up with Sucio. Our moms put us in a stroller together and rolled us down Tremont Avenue while they smoked weed. We knew Sucio said he'd do it himself, but like . . . what if he changed his mind? Even the baddest motherfucker gets weak in the balls staring down the barrel, the steel of a .357, a Glock 'n' shit. But Mermaid said there were lots of guns wandering the city, ready for work.

But what if we hired a gun, how do we know he's really a professional (and not just money grubby)? And what if the mamma jamma fucked up and just grazed Sucio's skull or some shit and the next we know Sucio is stumbling around the grass, bleeding in a world of pain? After that he might come out of a hospital, wearing a baby bib and dribbling oatmeal 'n' shit. He might end up like a lot of guys who took the drive-bys in the spine, and now they shit in their pants all day in a wheelchair stuck in some welfare hotel. I'm not buying into that shit.

We all agreed that Sucio had big balls and he got to do himself. But then Froggy reminded us: "By not getting a shooter, you're leaving the whole party up to Sucio. That sucks the dick!"

But then I had an idea (after I told Froggy not to get loud with us 'n' shit). What if we set something up? That way, if Sucio got rubbery in the nuts, we could have like a booby trap. We could tape the gun, aimed at Sucio's head, to a tree and put a long rubber band to the trigger and tie the band to Tommy's dog. That way, when the little bugger jumped for Sucio's meat 'n' shit, the rubber band would snap, WHACK, BANG, and we got us a fucking party, word to the mother.

Finally, the shit was settled. We were ready to do the invitations. Pookie was worried about the wording. What if it gets into the wrong hands? It's against the law and if they find out, they'll come down on us. But even if it's against the law, I figure we got us a right to do it because Sucio is *our* boy. His ass belongs to us. And he's fucked up and we can't have fucking up no more.

We all decided that the invitations should be written in gangsta so anybody from the law will go like, *Come to a Waxin* . . . like *whassup*? And Pookie says she'll even add a little of her own money. She'll pay for some fancy lettering. And we all agreed. Money should not matter no more!

Like yo, I said, we're Sucio's best friends and if we can't treat the boy right, then *damn*, what the hell is the world coming to? I said we should let Sucio drink all the wine he wants and take as many drugs as he likes (even if it's a waste of a good high).

Right on, said Zoom-O. Even Froggy and Pookie gave me a satisfied look for the first time.

Like, the party went off real good. We had plenty of peeps and everybody laughed. The deejay rocked the instruments, bumping Sucio's favorite tracks. Some girls danced for Sucio, and he sat there, not even moving. Pookie spun in circles under a leafy tree.

When I finally slapped the gun in Sucio's hand, that nigga was buggin'. Pookie gave him a loosie and a few blunts. He smoked his brains out, and then he took two shits behind a tree.

Froggy was going mad crazy. That night, he was Sucio's dog. But every time he tossed out another shovel of dirt from the ditch, already down six feet, he mumbled about "forty-drinkin niggas that don't give a fuck if they live or die."

Zoom-O kept yelling, "Now we keepin' it real. Dig, motherfucker."

It was getting dark and I was worried. All that waiting around with the loaded gun, Sucio started flossin' and making plans with Pookie on the DL, telling her how she'd be his shorty for life. He was fucking up again.

"Froggy, get your ass out of the grave," I said.

Then I stepped on the deejay's shit and told everybody to recognize.

"It's time to pull the trigger," I said.

Sucio gave me a grateful smile. And Pookie was proud of her man as he fell facefirst into the dirt—the motherfucker had balls. He didn't ask for a chair, a blindfold, or nothing. He just went—WHACK, BANG.

. . .

But now, like these assholes from Queens are still pissed off that we stole their money 'n' shit for Sucio's party. The other day, like, I was out by the park with Tommy's dog when I was surrounded by them.

I knew the biggest one, the loudest one, who called himself D.B., the one with the tattoos like spiders up in my face telling me he got this personal beef. That asshole was dipped in black leather and gold chains. He had wraparound shades, silver.

Suddenly one of his boyz starts going on about this guy Colby, how he shot this little kid, and how they hung that motherfucker—and now they'd be happy to hang me.

This guy took out a long rope and pointed to some trees in the park, and said how easy it would be to see me swinging. But like I told that D.B., I said, "Whassup? I'm not into this shit."

He said, "It's not the money, you know, it's like Colby, it's like *the idea* that you stole—that you fucked with us."

Which is when I tried to educate these boys about the whole shit, and how they got it wrong.

"Brothers," I said. "You don't get it. It's like, when you fuck up, you hang yourself."

But personally, I added, "I'm not into this killing-myself shit." And the next thing I knew I was running for the trees with Tommy's dumb-ass dog yapping and jumping at my meat, and that posse at my heels.

The Nobody

Yo, Yo—this is Crusader talking, Crusader de Chato, from South Central, where Reginald Denny got his butt whipped, big time—and I want you to know that this is a big day in my life because I'm cutting school to begin my work as a writer. Well, not exactly a writer. I hate writing. I'm a REwriter. I REwrite on fences, on buildings, and on anything that moves—eight to eighty, blind, cripple, or crazy; if it can't walk, I'll drag it. I'd put my tag on a rat's ass if it would stick.

So, I write my name which isn't really my name. It sure ain't the name I got from my mom. I want no part of that witch. I write my gang name, CHATO, which means cat face. That's the name of the boy I like. He got a flat nose, like a squishy kitten, ohhh, so cute, makes my knees like syrup just thinking about kissing that little brown pooch. You know that's a Mexican name. Chato is a Mexican boy. He got that name from his lang*widge*, which is Mexican. I'm not scared to say I don't know his widge. But I don't think it's better than English. I don't like English and those dumb teachers. Why can't I make up my own widge? %$@#! ★★&^%. That would be so cool, like yo!

Not that I'm English or anything just because I speak it. Mom says I'm a crazy salad. Part African, Cherokee, and Italian. The Italian part cracks me up because I eat pizza every Thursday. Mom says the reason we got Italian is that this explorer Christopher Columbus parked his boat in Cuba when they had them slaves there. Mom says them ladies looked so hot and them Talians be so horny they jumped ship and started bumping the uglies, hear what I'm saying? That's why my last name is Coolio, which sounds like PolyO, that Italian cheese, mozzarella. You eat that shit? (Chato I want you so bad, you so hot, *carajo.*) But I ask my mom: If them horny *Talians* parked that ship in Cuba, like you say, how long was it before they had to go back and put quarters in the parking meter? My mom, she doesn't get the joke because she sees that I'm flunking school big time and so she doesn't know when I'm dumb or just playing with her head. I'm sor-reee—okay?

After Crusader de Chato I write "de Leon." That's the street I live on, the one that gave my gang its name, the Lions. But now they're gone: Alphabet was shotgun blasted by Slug. Nice guys, but my boy "Alpha" was doing the stinky finger with Slug's woman. Then there was Bleachy. He talked too much to dope-dealing pigs and ended up in Internal Affairs. They put his butt in witness protection . . . somewhere on Mars.

But I still got the old arsenal in my basement behind the boiler. I dig it up when I get lonely. I got the Glocks and the semiautomatics with fresh bullet clips in them. I still got the brass knuckles, even though nobody ever got that close and lived. Now everything is mine. I'm the last Lion, Crusader. But I'm glad to know I got this stuff in case some sucker plays with my head. Then I'll have to put a hole in him like I got a hole. I'll give the sucker a pussy—word up!

Anyway, today started out like every day. The toilet bowl made its usual sucking sound like an asshole blowing in instead of out. Then my Pop hacked so hard, green stuff shot from his nose. He dripped his frog scum right into the sink where I got to brush my teeth. Then he yells that it's seven o'clock, so I yell back, "So what! I quit school." Just like that, I decided. That's me, straight up in your face.

"Don't you want to be a nurse no more?" says Pop.

Old Pop likes to play with me. He thinks he's so funny. Next time I make a plan in the world I'm not telling him.

"What happened? You don't want to make money and take care of me when I get old?"

"Patzzo, patzzo," I say in the Talian I learned at the pizza shop.

"If you quit school," says Pop, "then you better marry one of them Compton Boyz, one of them gangsta stars with a recording contract bigger than his rap sheet."

"You know," I say, "I'm not just quitting school today. I'm quitting this dump. I'm never coming back here again."

I screamed right in his face. But he just went into the kitchen and made a big noise with the egg scrambler. I could get killed and he wouldn't kick it. So I went to my room and laid in the bed until Pop left. When I woke up, it was after lunch. Lately I can sleep forever, so I get up and put on my crotch-pulling pants, my leather vest with the Madonna bra, the silver studs for nipples. I got this feeling today is going to be my big day—something like that.

I had to wait for my food at McDonald's. Some kid got sick and threw up on the checkout machine. There's always a bottle-sucker vomiting his guts out at McDonald's and isn't it always the fat ones? They eat anything—blind, cripple, or crazy. But when they're born everybody is so polite, saying how cute they look. But they're not so cute when they squirt themselves all over your Quarter Pounder. Sometimes my mom asks me if she should have another baby, but I warn her: If she does, I'll squeeze it hard when she's not looking. And talk about *looking*? My mom used to be good-looking. Now I don't like to look at her. She got purple veins running up and down her legs. She got all swollen up like a pastry bag of pus.

I finally get my food, but I hold my nose while I eat since that kid stunk up the place. For a minute I think I'm going to school, but then

I remember. I leave my backpack for the busboy, who winks as I go bye-bye.

Every time I walk down my street I feel bad about what they've done. Houses that once had garden hoses out front are nothing but vacant lots, filled with piss-stained socks and empty crack vials. Those fires, after Rodney King, turned everything into ash. The shopping mall that once had these cool rubber palm trees is all boarded up now. And a new building they started was stopped, leaving this big pit where they dug out what was supposed to be a basement—a play space. I hope you never live in a place where everybody goes stupid over some crazy cops who got us burned out.

My first stop is a gate outside my block. There's this sign again, a "T" wrapped across a skull, which is the mark of the Turbans, a gang that would love to wipe me out. So I take out my spray can and REwrite my name on it (even though I know these assholes will come back tonight to put it right). In the old days, nobody would do this. But these days nobody respects anybody because everybody got a gat, a gun, to drop you in a heartbeat. Fact is, one day these punks will catch me and that'll be the end of "Crusader de Chato de Leon."

So I go down the side streets like a fog, like a ghost. But to let everyone know I'm alive, I write my name all over the billboard outside a parking lot. A lot of names you see are messed up, but not after I REwrite them. I take my time. I'm real neat, like I learned from my second-grade teacher, Mr. Kramer. If you write nice, he said, people will take you seriously. He was real sweet to me. He always walked me to the bus stop whenever somebody was out to knife me. I think he wanted to take me home. He called me his "little lamb." I never went, though I owe him a lot.

You should see my tags, all curvy and tight like my hips. Everybody thinks so, though I'm not sure about Chato. He got so many tags all over town I'm always REwriting his mess. Like, he thinks he's VOP (Voice of the Projects), but I know the truth behind his writing (which I can't tell you just now). Anyway—

I fixed Chato's mess and then I thought maybe I should go by and see if anybody I knew was outside my school. But then I got into the mood to REwrite some more. I went to a Korean store and stole myself a box of Day-Glo markers. Then I went down the freeway, scribbling all the way, wondering if I should really piss off that Chato, if I should do more than fix up his name, write, maybe: *Chato is my Man*, or *Chato ain't Chicano*. Wouldn't that be a pisser? What if Chato turned out to be a hard loaf to cut, a white bread? Man, some *hermanos* be really pissed that some milky messed in the *barrio*.

But then, I figured that was too mean (even if Chato kept ignoring me). I didn't want to rock his world so hard he'd fall off. So I just went on my way until something big hit me: I tagged Chato's name to the Golden Arches. Then I saw Alicea's Funeral Home with these big white coffins and silver urns in the window. I snuck up on one of those black limos and tagged Chato on a back wheel. Afterwards, I wondered if this was bad luck. But then I figured, since Chato's gonna get shot someday anyway, like everybody else, he could at least have himself the best damn funeral in Los Angeles. I think he's gonna be happy when he sees what I've done.

Talk about funerals. Suddenly I catch the Turbans coming off a ramp, low-riding in a black Cherokee, the gold in their teeth as shiny as their chrome wheel covers. I'm not scared of dying myself, but these bastards can't shoot straight, and if I take a bullet in the back, if I end up spinal-tapped in a wheelchair with this yellow stuff dried in the corners of my mouth, I know my Pop is gonna wheel me into a closet and slam the door. Tie a black ribbon to my arm.

I fast step into Marco's. It's one of these telethon charities, a place where wannabe cops make sure kids got a safe zone in the hood, a nice joint to play games. They got a color TV going all day and a pool table balanced on a pile of old car batteries. After losing a few games, I get bored and so I write my tag on the cue sticks. It looks real funny and shit. Everybody starts cracking up until big old Marco shows his face. He's always spying on us from somewhere. He took me to his office, like I was trembling in my panties—yeah.

"So, Crusader," he says, drumming his fingers on his desk. "Now that your gang is gone, who's gonna watch your back?"

"Don't need it," I say. "Don't give a fuck."

"Uh-huh," he says. "I keep hearing about you. Why don't you let me get you into a museum school? They got graffiti classes. The mayor sponsors it."

"School is boring. I hate it and I don't care nothing about art. I write."

"Chato is making a name for himself. I hear he's gonna quit messing with private property. I hear he's working on a mural in a train station. It's like a job—you get paid."

"What's Chato got to do with anything?"

"I hear you're making him famous all over town, but now that he wants to quit he's not happy about you rewriting his tags."

"Chato? Train stations? Ha! Talk about a wreck. His stuff looks like shit. Besides, it's not him writing, believe me. He's bullshitting."

"Just why are you doing this, Crusader? You want to be a somebody, too?"

"No, I don't want to be nobody."

"Then why are you here? You want to make new friends? Why aren't you in school?"

"I'm not going back."

"It's the Turbans? You seen them at the school today?"

"I mess with their tags, so what?"

"Mess is the right word. What you do is like a cat spraying itself on a tree. What's with that?"

"Who you calling a cat? I don't got to take shit from you or anybody, not even my pop calls me that. You're nothing, you hear me? You're really a nobody."

I told him right in his face. I let the brown out. I cursed him real good, but I doubt he listened. He's one of those that gets paid to keep on talking, *talk, talk*, and show you all kinds of applications, tell you about all kinds of programs, always trying to get you to sign up for something, offering you an AIDS test and condoms and shit. When he finally ran out of gas, I got up and left. From that day on I swore that place was GAD—Good as Dead.

Back on the street, along the freeway, it was real dark, but I could still follow my trail to where I began. It was real nice to see my tags in the flickering headlights, all lit up and quivering like they was on a big movie screen up there in Hollywood Hills. But at Sucio's bodega I stopped in my tracks, stone solid. Around Chato's tag someone drew a red skull. Then they put my name *Crusader* inside the toothless grin. Straight up, I was pissed off big time. If it's Chato that did this (my little coconut), what kind of guy does this to a girl, especially a girl that always puts her heart into her work? And if it wasn't Chato, I better move in the slow lane.

And Chato, that's what it turned out to be. I caught up with him by the old construction site. There he was in the shadows hidden behind some burned-out cars spraying red skulls over what I'd RE-written, his name, which I fixed up today. I snuck up on him real quiet, my heart going flippity-flop. Crazy ideas got into my head, making my body shake.

Then he turned around before I could get on his neck. He looked at me real hard. I took off down the alley, but in forty feet he was on me. He grabbed my markers, but I whipped them behind my back. He reached around and tried pulling my fingers open. His hands were sweaty like mine so he couldn't get a grip. Besides, I was squirming and kicking, and we fell down and on top of each other, over a rail and into the bottom of this pit. Lucky it was all mud.

I could feel Chato's arms around me with everything he got. His breath was on my cheek. He twisted against me and I started giggling. Be honest, I don't like wrestling with boys. They fight dirty. He bit my neck and when I went to scratch his nose, he got a good hold of my markers.

"What right you got using my name," he said, all mad. "Did I give you permission?"

"Permission," I said. "You're so dumb. I didn't take your name. I've been taking your story, your whole fucking life and making it mine."

"Why, what makes you special to swipe my tag and shit?"

" 'Cause you're a nobody. Chato ain't real. That's just something you write to make everybody think you're somebody."

"So, why mess with me?"

" 'Cause I'm a nobody too. And just today, I nearly told everyone about you. I nearly spread it all over the freeway, like a billboard."

"You'd do that to me?"

"Actually, I wouldn't care—Chato. But maybe you and me can have a lot of fun? Maybe we can go REwriting together. Nobody got to know who we are."

"Fool everybody," said Chato. "I write over the Turbans' tag?"

Suddenly, I saw that Chato had a big smile. He came up close and put his hand on mine, like sexy; he pressed my markers into my hand. I think he was about to say yes, that REwriting would be the bomb.

We could go around holding hands in the dark, talking for hours under a tree in the park. I could teach him everything I knew about being a neater, a better, writer.

But then he started telling me that he had this "rep" to protect, blah-blah, and if his boyz scoped him hanging out with a chick, they'd be cracking on him 24/7. He took his hand from mine.

"Crusader," he said, "even if you tell everybody about me, for real, being with a girl is a lot worse. You gotta step off, serious."

"Step off?" I said. "Who you talking to, you no-count, lame-to-the-wood sissy boy."

I called him everything I knew. (You know I got a mouth.) Then he tried to spit in my face but . . . you slow, you blow. I was too fast. He missed. So I took my markers and tried to hit him in the face. But then he was quick and gone down the street.

I just drifted over to the park near my house, which is a good place to sit under the stars. As I sat there, I hated everybody and everything, but the one thing I didn't hate, the one thing I could see, was my best work still under the biggest street lamp in the city. It was my tag, *Chato de Leon*, in gold letters. And next to it: CRUSADER LOVES CHATO. I just stood there under a tree watching people look at it when they stopped, people strolling in the park who knew something about romance and holding hands.

There was one guy that got out of his sports car, a beeper in his hand and chains on his neck. He stopped to use a phone booth. He saw my name and smiled at me, his teeth capped in silver. His face was sweet. I didn't want to stare, but he kept looking at my tag like he fell in love with it. He wanted to take me for a ride, I could tell. He'd put out his hand and off we'd go to the Beverly Hills Motel, and everything.

I almost said "Take me" to that guy. But I didn't say nothing. I was left on that corner with my gold marker and my clothes all muddy. But I didn't sweat it. I knew one day I'd end up like a movie star. All I needed was to steal some new markers when the sun came up. Then Chato and me would be famous all over again, as long as I made like a ghost and made sure the Turbans didn't get me—as long as I stayed a mystery, fooling everybody.

Cleopatra

Every pothole on the Cross Bronx Expressway must've been hit, rattling the steel-caged windows on the blue city bus, its shock absorbers long gone, threadbare like the green seats, the vinyl split at the seams like so many pods burst wide open. Daryl was busy sticking chewed gum into the vinyl cracks, his butt bouncing hard every time the driver, handcuffs dangling from his gun belt, braked over another crater and cursed his bad luck.

The courthouse was right off the expressway, the bus fan blowing hot air on Daryl, the humidity a killer. His long-sleeved shirt made the heat even worse. He was the last on the bus. The streets seemed unusually quiet. The baby strollers that always lined up outside the abandoned buildings first thing in the morning (while moms rushed in to get something for their heads) were all gone. It was too quiet on the old street.

The driver handed Daryl a brown bag, his leather coat still balled inside, his house keys still in his pocket, his wallet with the same twenty bucks—all that he had the night he was arrested six years back.

A stuffed seal with a red ribbon around its neck was also inside, still inside its wrapper, left over from a McDonald's Happy Meal.

The driver unlocked the doors, fumbling with a big ring of keys. He barely glanced up when Daryl dropped the brown bag and asked if he could put it under his good arm; the other one was just a lump with a steel rod inside. If Daryl could get some public money, the prison doctor said, he might have a shot at a digital hand with moving fingers. One thing for sure: Daryl would never again wrap his trigger finger around a heater, a .38-caliber semiautomatic cronz (which had got him locked up in the first place).

Maybe it was too hot. Everybody got crazy with the sun beating down, and they went inside. Even the courthouse looked shut, just the air conditioners cranking out cool air on the sills of the darkened windows. That must've been what got the bus driver in such a hurry to see Daryl out of his face.

Usually the guards made a little speech before they set you free. And if this guy were a prick, Daryl would've said something too. But he actually did Daryl a solid, taking him from outside the prison gate, upstate, where nobody was coming for him.

For a homeboy with a badge, a paycheck nigga (as Daryl called him), he wasn't a talker. Usually these brothers used that church voice to tell young convicts, "Son, you gotta leave that thug life behind, leave it to them gangsta stars with the big recording contracts. Those suckers sing about shooting people, but you ever see them do the time?"

These righteous brothers were always dissin' the rappers, swearing that when the made-for-TV-gangstas ended up in jail, like Tupac Shakur, the real thugs ended up renting their assholes by the hour. That's what they said. But forget it—if these guards thought you looked even a little bit interested in what they preached, they'd stick you in a jail cell with one of them bow-tie boys real quick, them pictures of the Honorable Reverend Farrakhan bearing down on you until you raised your right hand and took that Million Dollar pledge, sweating:

> I pledge from this day forward I will not
> raise my hand with a knife, or a gun to beat, cut,
> or shoot any member of my family or any human
> being except in self-defense.
> I will never engage in the abuse of children, little
> boys or little girls—

Usually Daryl hated to hear all that stuff, but he was kind of surprised that this guard didn't even take one last crack at him. Daryl waved good-bye to him, forgetting that he had the brown bag under his arm. Everything fell out when it hit the ground, the McDonald's toy nearly rolling into a storm drain.

When Daryl stood up, the bag under his good arm again, he saw some little girls walking on the other side of the street. He liked the little girls, liked the look of them better than the little boys, who were always kicking each other, acting like Power Rangers until their eyes watered and the green stuff ran from their noses. He liked the look of little girls.

But he was no longer allowed in their world. He couldn't be where they were—not anymore. He couldn't face the terror of their little laughs. Just watching them cross the street was more frightening than anything he'd faced in jail. He couldn't deal with it, how everything on his street suddenly looked more dangerous, no matter how much pretty paint they put on the burned-out buildings. He watched the little girls with their backpacks, the Little Mermaids bobbing on their backs like so many party balloons ready to go pop—the sun going down behind the projects, the playground shuttered behind barbed wire.

He considered stepping into a store to buy some candy, some enticing treats. He looked into the window and studied the chocolate section, the Kit-Kat bars, the Hershey's in their bright wrappers in neat stacks. He always liked those candy stacks, but now he didn't trust them, trying to reach up with one arm—limp and heavy—he didn't trust them anymore, up too high like a lot of things, too easy to knock down.

Why did she expect any help from him?

Pablo gave Wanda a sponge cake in a grocery box shaped like a heart, the thick red cream stuck to its sides. The M&M topping had already melted and streaked blue veins across the happy face in white cream. Wanda didn't think it was cute or anything.

"This ain't Valentine's Day, you fool."

She could have had a Welcome Home at a Discovery Zone or something like that. Instead Pablo the Fool went to Blockbuster Video and brought back some more porno films, which they watched, his hand on her shoulder, while he whispered, all choked up, "Baby, me so horny, sittin' in the dark, my dick all hard."

But the films only made Wanda more aware of what she had lost. Besides Daryl gone all these years, her little girl, her three-year-old Cleopatra, had been killed. Watching all that in and out on the screen, all that slobbering, only made Wanda think of trying again, of having Daryl give her a new baby.

Pablo had hoped Daryl would flunk the parole hearing, thinking

Wanda would've been desperate enough to finally give it up. But with Daryl back, Wanda looked around and it was clear: All she could see and talk about were all those places Cleo used to play, like the hide-and-seek under the broken armchair where she peed so often there was always this warm, damp spot that never seemed to quit. Even now Wanda touched it and imagined it was damp.

"Wanda," said Pablo, "I'm really crazy mad about the cake getting messed up and shit."

"No you ain't," said Wanda. "And you better get going—go out the window and down the fire escape so you don't bump into Daryl."

"But nothing happened, not even some stinky finger."

Wanda wanted to scream.

"That's what pisses me off," she said. "You men act like dogs. Why don't you get one of them meat-market bitches to suck you off?"

"Why don't you stop being so scared, bitch? Sooner or later you'll give it up."

"Well, later is better. And if you don't go, you'll see—bitch yourself."

Wanda was thinking about that egg she just saw in this porno movie. This woman stuck it, hard boiled, into this guy's mouth . . . then she taped his lips and bound his wrists. She held his nose until he turned so blue his prick nearly sprung off. If Wanda only had that egg now, she told Pablo, she knew what she'd do with it.

Pablo said he didn't like eggs. They had a way of cracking themselves. But he got the message, even though he'd be back, even if it meant fucking with Daryl. He climbed out the window, muttering, "My dick so hard."

"Nah, nah," Bobalou yelled from behind the counter. "Can't be!"

But the guys at the pinball machines in the back didn't hear.

"Daryl." Bobalou gave him a big hug. "How you holding up, brother?"

"Awright, I'm okay," said Daryl. Bobalou had the candy store ever since he got his GI loan, since Vietnam fried his brains. "I'm okay."

"Man, we heard you got paroled."

"Judge figured I killed a drug dealer, whatever. Figured it's a war."

"Whatever, my man. Just look at you. Hey, lookit!" Bobalou called to the back.

Pablo was the last to turn from his game. The others had their hands all over Daryl. Froggy, the youngest, was the most impressed.

"Daryl, what are you doing here," said Pablo. "You supposed to be at Wanda's, remember?"

Pablo gripped Daryl's hand on reflex, but came up with a stump instead.

"Damn," Pablo said. "Them bullets fucked you right up."

"How come they didn't hook you up with one of those digital hands?" said Froggy. "Like in them Coke commercials?"

"Yeah," said Bobalou. "You can be the first bionic brother on the block. I've seen them hands in 'Nam; brothers could rip a steel plate off an oil drum. How'd you like that around your neck, eh Pablo?"

Pablo scowled. "Bobalou, why you gotta play with me?"

" 'Cause," said Bobalou. "You like games, don't you?"

"Yo, yo—brothers," said Daryl, rolling down his long sleeves. "Chill out and tell me about Wanda, somebody, you seen how she looks?"

"She was in here the other day," said Pablo.

"She looks okay," said Bobalou. "She should be fucked by now, considering Cleo, on drugs, or booze."

"I couldn't blame her," said Daryl.

"So what we gonna do?" said Froggy. "Now you're back."

"Yeah." Everybody seemed eager for a mission. Daryl was always the big brain, setting up the right moves, making sure that everyone on his turf kept the money circulating, making sure the pig tolls were paid, the cops chilling.

"Look in the bag," said Daryl.

Froggy pulled out Daryl's old leather.

There was a time when they all wore the same jackets and called themselves the Leather Boyz. No one fucked with them. They did all kinds of sick shit together, especially him and Pablo. When they were kids their favorite game was punching old ladies in the back, making them gag so hard their teeth fell out. "Kick out the canes!" They laughed so hard.

"Shit. You still got it," said Froggy. Everybody passed the jacket around.

"You still got yours?" asked Daryl.

"Nah," said Pablo. "That style's been tired out."

"You mean, we're tired," said Froggy. "Bobalou, you should take down that African flag behind the counter and tack this up. This is black pride, motherfucker."

"Fuck you," said Bobalou. "You so stupid. But Daryl, it's up to him. Pride ain't got nothing to do with it."

"Personally, I don't give a shit," said Daryl. "You niggers do what you want."

"Then why you stopped in here?" said Pablo.

"It was so quiet and I was wondering. You know, we made a mistake with Cleopatra. We should've had a small coffin, a grave; instead, we had her cremated, you know, burned."

"Check yourself out. *Quiet.* Wasn't quiet when they capped your ass and your kid."

"And I hear," said Froggy, "those guys you sent to prison, they got some kids, some little brothers, they got family just waiting for your ass, that's what I hear, and it won't be quiet when they drop you in a heartbeat."

"Why do you think it's quiet? Since you been gone, we been taking the heat for you—six years, motherfucker. You set the shit up. It's quiet 'cause we let it be quiet."

"But they're in prison," said Daryl. "Those guys."

"I know that. What I'm saying is, we got to go for their little brothers and sisters, and cap the little fuckers right in the Pampers if we got to," said Pablo.

"Come on," said Daryl, "shooting kids?"

"KIDS MY ASS," said Froggy. "You got to get those little nipple suckers before they get grown up. 'Cause then those little pricks will be strapped. It'll be harder to drop 'em, hear what I'm saying?"

"When you was in prison, why do you think they dropped Cleo?" said Pablo. "Everybody knew she was gonna take after you—and be on their ass straight out of the sixth grade and shit."

"Well, if them little kids are looking for me, then you got nothing to worry about. If some kid wants to burn my ass, let 'em rock my world—hear what I'm saying?" said Daryl.

He rolled another long, sweaty sleeve down his tube, his arm. He picked up his brown bag and let the front door slam behind him.

"Fuck if we care!" Pablo yelled at his back. "You gimp motherfucker. One-arm piece of shit."

"Be cool," said Bobalou. "Man lost his girl." He hung Daryl's jacket behind the candy counter.

Everybody watched Daryl from behind the chocolates. Daryl in the blazing sun, the only asshole not walking in the shade, right in the middle of the day. His lame arm hung at his side, dangled like a club, a heavy thing that seemed to pull his shoulder to the street, threatened to topple him into the gutter.

Pablo turned to his boy, Froggy.

"I should've banged that Wanda, that dumb bitch. I should've busted her pussy wide open. I respected that motherfucker."

"Yeah but now he's back," said Froggy. "Now you'll be singing 'Sittin' home with my dick all hard' for *real*."

"Yeah, well," said Pablo. "Once he gets that digital hand all Wanda be getting is a piece of cold steel upside her twat—*yo*."

"Word up," said Froggy. "Then she'll be singing a new song: 'Once my baby is digital, he'll play with my clitoral.' " He burst out laughing so hard he sprayed spit onto the store window.

"Fuckin' slobs," said Bobalou. "Why you got to talk like that, all turdy. You ain't got no fucking heart, none of you."

"You know what?" said Pablo, reaching behind his back, under his hoodie. "You're getting on my nerves."

"Oh yeah," said Bobalou. "On your nerves? Which ones? Show me and I'll fix 'em for you."

That's when Pablo shoved his gun under Bobalou's nose. But Bobalou just turned away, as easy as Slick Rick, Grand Master Flash. He turned to his CD and pumped up the volume. It was James Brown.

"The Big Payback!" crooned Bobalou right back in Pablo's face as Froggy took the gun from Pablo's hand and put it under his shirt. "James Brown, the Man!"

Daryl didn't expect it, Maxine opening the door. She came over to Wanda's to talk. They were best friends since high school. Now Maxine worked in an electronics store selling beepers to b-boys with fat

Nikes. She always wore too much makeup and skirts too short. She had to take care of her own kids now.

"I can't believe it," said Maxine, touching Daryl's cheek. "Baby."

She threw her arms around him.

"Yo, Maxine," said Daryl, feeling tired. "Where's Wanda?"

"She saw you from the window. She's in the room. It's too much."

"The guys thought she looked okay."

"The other day," said Maxine, "she wanted to give me Cleo's clothes for Sabrina. I told her it's not a good idea. She'll keep seeing them."

"I hear you," said Daryl. He looked around the apartment. Everything was just the same, like six years ago. He took out the McDonald's seal, still in its wrapper, and left it on the stain under the big chair.

"You always too much, Daryl," said Maxine quietly, trying to rub back a tear.

"So," said Daryl. "When are you getting the *rock?*"

"Soon as she wakes up."

"Will it take hours to find someone we can trust? I'm on probation, hear what I'm saying?"

"Don't worry," joked Maxine, going out the door. "You won't end up a headliner, 'Homecoming Up in Smoke.' "

Daryl quietly unlatched the bedroom door with a penknife. It was dark, the shades drawn, Wanda still under a sheet.

"Hey baby, I'm here. It's our big day."

He felt slightly ill from the heat. He hadn't eaten yet or had anything to drink, and the room was like a sauna, the windows locked.

"The big days are over," he heard her mumble, her face buried in the pillow. "Once I believed in them, but now I know—"

Daryl saw that a cake with red cream was stuck in a trash can next to the bed.

"You fixed up a party? Is it because I'm late?"

"No, I gotta be truthful." She sat up now and buried her head on his shoulder, not flinching from the mechanical joint. "I can't do any better. I'm glad you're out, Daryl."

Daryl leaned back and lay in the bed.

"We gotta face the truth," he said. "Whatever it is, we gotta be honest when we know it. While I was gone, whatever it is, we'll face it."

Just then there was a knock at the front door. Somehow Maxine had found a crack dealer who delivered. He put five vials in Daryl's hand and left. Back in the room, Daryl said, "Remember when we was young, Wanda? I made some crazy cash, and we'd be going to the movies all day, your hands in the dark, in my pants, just squeezing?"

"I know you liked that sex in public," she said. "Now my face is falling."

Daryl put some crack into the pipe he got from the dealer. He felt a little nervous, excited. He'd been off the stuff so long—if some neighbors smelled the rock cooking, if he got caught now, if they busted down his door, they'd drag him off to jail.

"Remember," said Daryl, holding the flame over the pipe, drawing in, "how we'd lay up in here, ears straining, listening for little Cleo, hoping she didn't wake up too early, our heads still busted from some party?"

But now, for the first time, they were alone in the apartment together. They stared toward the living room as if something would stir. He could still see little Cleo crawling around under the chair, her Pampers leaky, all gummy and yellow, sucking on her thumb, the room filled with the familiar and comforting smell, the smoke like breakfast cooking. But now Daryl wasn't sure if it was the crack he was smelling or the pipe burning. He sucked some more, throwing his head back, eyes closed. He handed Wanda the pipe.

She put some more rock in the bowl while Daryl held the match over it. She had the sensation of being sucked into a drain and tumbled headlong into pipes rushing with cold water. It felt so good she almost couldn't stand it. She held onto Daryl, tight in her arms. She had to have another bowl as soon as possible.

It wouldn't go away. She just stopped in that playground to put Cleo in the sprinkler, for like a minute, to cool her off. The air-conditioning in the McDonald's went out, so it was no use hanging out there any longer. Cleo had woken up early, before the sun, shit caked to her ass and piss leaking from her diaper. She'd been cranky all night and bitching and screeching from the heat rash between her fat little thighs, her little mouth all gummy and trembling with spit, and now Wanda just wanted some time to kick back and settle herself before they'd be back in her hot room.

"One second, Cleo-pie. Mom's gettin' a nice surprise."

Wanda dug in her baby bag for a snack, a little candy. Cleo had already wandered off to the mermaid pool, a blue basin with a porpoise fountain like a shower massage hung on a wire to spray water over Cleo's head.

"Mom's comin', my sweetest pie, yes, she is."

Cleo was giggling and laughing. She scooped handfuls of water into the air, tossing it up like she could catch it coming down. Then Wanda turned away to look deeper into her bag for that little treat. *Blam, bam*, she heard the gun. She might've seen something if she hadn't turned away. She might've been able to know something more than what the police said, acting like it was her fault, saying it was just like the neighborhood kids (wasn't it?), the boyz doing what they do, just like her boyfriend who got himself shot.

But it should've been her blood swirling in that drain beneath that horrible porpoise, its beak spraying cold water, washing her baby away. "It should've been me," she told the cops.

When it was done, they were drenched in sweat, their pupils wide, hearts beating irregularly. They went through the five vials. Daryl giggled uncontrollably while Wanda kept pulling at his penis, sticking her tongue in his ear. He wouldn't give it up. He didn't want to.

"Come on," Wanda said. "I just want to get pregnant. You can do that—even if the idea is fucked up."

Daryl didn't find anything funny anymore. He closed his eyes, the harder she pulled, shaking his head side to side, "No, no."

Then he felt like he had to potty. He got up from the bed, his head all mushy, his arm awkward and heavy, like a club, and it spun him around and he flipped back and fell onto the trash can, putting out his good hand to break his fall, only to get it cut crushing an empty vial that was on the floor. He had glass in him now and the red pastry cream was splattered everywhere. The sheets were covered with cake, and the blood down his hand got on the pillows and on Wanda as she stumbled up to the bed.

The next few hours were spent sitting in cream while Wanda used a tweezers to pull the glass shards from Daryl's swollen palm. Now they were sure the neighbors had called the cops. When he fell, his arm, his club, hit the wall so hard it sounded like a shotgun blast or something. Now he was fucked for sure.

That's why they didn't answer the doorbell. Whoever was ringing, it couldn't be good news. They shrank to the floor slowly and cowered as far under the box springs as possible. Wanda pulled the sheets over their heads as well. Daryl couldn't help but relieve himself right there. The bell kept ringing and they were sure any minute the cops would bust in, guns drawn, badges pinned to DEA windbreakers.

But it was Maxine who finally came up the fire escape and banged on the window. Daryl's mouth was completely parched now. His tongue felt like ash. He could barely speak, convincing Maxine that he was stoned out of his brain. His mouth moved, but nothing came out.

"Back to the slammer!" Maxine howled, realizing that she'd scared the hell out of them. "Now hand over the pipe."

When Wanda woke up, Maxine was in the bed between them.

She hadn't even bothered to shake the cake crumbs off the sheet. Maxine was right into it, work clothes and all.

"So, how's it going?" she asked while sucking on a bowl.

"Great," said Wanda, taking the pipe. "We're having a baby."

"How'd you get pregnant so fast, girlfriend?"

"If you're thinking about Pablo, he never pulled my panties, no way."

"Then what're you thinking about?"

"He keeps going no, but I'm having me a kid," said Wanda, running her hand over Daryl's sleeping head.

In the weeks that followed, Daryl found ticket stubs in the laundry bag. Wanda was out these days, all day. He spent his time at the Public Assistance agency. He didn't have time for the movies. Bobalou kept telling him. If he wanted, he'd move out the pinball machines and let Daryl have the back room. "Set up a shop," said Bobalou. Daryl had learned VCR repair in prison.

Then Daryl ran into Pablo and Wanda in the hallway, behind the stairs next to the boiler room. "Get fucked if you want," said Daryl. He tried to stay calm. They had to face the truth, whatever it was. Now that Daryl didn't get hard, no matter how much she yanked, who could blame her? At night, her head nestled in his plastic armpit, they stared at the bedroom door, waiting for something to stir.

In the days that followed, Wanda heard more and more about Pablo going around and bragging that he'd nailed Daryl's woman.

"Wha-chu mean?" said Pablo, all defensive, as they sat in the dark movie theater.

"Don't you even think I'm into this because you some kind of wild man. This ain't about busting my pussy—it's about Daryl being disgusted."

"It's about the kid," said Pablo. "So what's that all about?"

"Don't you even talk about it. You ain't knocked me up, all this time, and you some kind of stud. So don't you ever mention Cleo to me—ever."

"Oh, yeah?" said Pablo. Then he acted no better than some stupid boyfriend. He hit Wanda in the face a few times. "And tell your man I'm coming for his ass, too."

When Daryl saw Wanda he didn't make a fuss about it. He wasn't sure what this would come to, but he knew it would come to something like this. He'd known Pablo, his main nigga, longer than Wanda. He always had the feeling that this sucker shot blanks, given they banged some of the same "bitches" (as Pablo called them), and the ones that got pregnant were the last ones with Daryl.

That night, Wanda and Daryl got into bed. He made love to her with his digital hand, with long slow strokes. Wanda kissed him passionately. Now and then they paused and stared off into the dark, each wondering if the other heard anything, something stirring just beyond the bedroom door. They would stop, lie quiet, and hold their breaths. Listening.

Faux Pas

"Turkey, you pissing me off."

The junkie who sat with his twin brother kept slamming the pawn up and down on the concrete chessboard in the park.

"Don't chip that piece," said Smiley. He had a high-pitched voice, like a girl, which didn't go right with his big body.

The junkies scratched themselves like they needed flea collars. Quinine in the heroin turned them flaky and brown. The only way to tell the twins apart was by their wounds. One had a bullet in his head. Everybody called him Slug. I figured Slug was already high, his eyeballs dripping and wet like his nose. Slug slammed the clock again, leaving Smiley only seconds to move. Smiley tried to concentrate but he couldn't. Slug kept sucking phlegm around his throat, and spitting under the chess table.

"Man, why you gotta be so noisy and nasty and shit," said Smiley with disgust. "I can't think."

He opened a pawn, two spaces, and took a knight on the adjacent space, sideways. He punched the clock, seconds now for Slug. Slug punched the clock back to Smiley.

"Yo, slow down," said Slug. "You can't do that. Pawns can take on the slant, not the side."

"Man," said Smiley, punching the seconds back to Slug. "I just did a foe-pah on your ass."

"Four-what?" said Slug, punching the clock back to Smiley. "You just making up shit so you can win."

Could Slug be that stupid? If you played chess in the park, if you laid down a bet, you better know the rules because the suckers that played here learned their shit in the jailhouse, played to get extra cigarettes and dinner forks shaved into shivs, played to survive a throwdown. This was serious.

Smiley tossed his chess book at Slug and told him to look up "foe-pah."

"I can't read," said Slug. "You do it."

The book was in my lap, the clock running. I found faux pas and after the third reading, Slug said I spoke too fast. He yanked the book from my hand and threw it to the ground. Smiley shook his head.

"Fuck four-pah," said Slug. His brother laughed his head off.

"Your time's run out," said Smiley.

"No," said Slug, "I think your ass is checked, motherfucker." He lifted his castle from behind the pawns and jumped it across the board, slamming it too hard on top of Smiley's king.

"Castle-pah!" said Slug, grinning. "We win, you pay."

"That's bullshit," I said.

"What," said Slug. "Look in the book. Can't you read?"

"Castles don't fly," said Smiley.

"Fuck," said Slug. "I say it's in the book."

Slug now laughed so hard he choked and coughed on his spit. Smiley sat back and calmly collected his chessmen.

"We're at that point, boys," he said.

"What?" said Slug, looking at me. "What's the nigger saying?"

Smiley leaned over the chessboard like he was grabbing for a piece. He came back across the table with a handful of Slug's hair, and Slug's body. Then he proceeded to use a full-fisted jab and a full range of motion to punch out Slug's mouth. One whack at a time, like Smiley was doing the sandbag, nothing making a sound except the blood squishing from Slug's head. I watched the whole thing and I noticed that the more Smiley punched, the calmer he got. He spoke one word slowly after each blow.

"You . . . got . . . to . . . learn," said Smiley, "when . . . you . . . get . . . to . . . a . . . point."

I felt, like, honored to witness this because it wasn't exactly brutal. Every blow to Slug's face was measured and snapped at the right angle, the right spot. Like, you could see that this was something that took

Smiley years of hard work and dedication, hours and hours of practice and focus.

In fact, there was something in Smiley's girl voice, something like a parent. He said he was sorry more than once. Then he dropped Slug, and grabbed his brother and smashed his face, too. But when it was over, Smiley didn't leave them on the ground. He stacked them on the table, carefully. He wrapped their arms around one another. It all felt and somehow looked like affection.

I scooped up the chess pieces that had fallen under the bench while Smiley wiped his bloody hands on a lunch napkin. When I got up, Smiley leaned over and kissed me on the top of my head. He did it like when I was a kid and I visited him at the farm.

It was always around the holidays. My mom rushed me out of bed on Sunday mornings. I was nine years old and rubbing my eyes and complaining about missing my cartoons. But if we missed the bus, my mom said, Smiley would be up there alone in the mountains with nothing but gray fields and haystacks, the deep snow all around. Usually I went back asleep on the bus and woke up to find myself on a dirt road that was nothing but trees to the sky and the bus smoking a white trail as it turned a sharp bend, leaving my mom and me to walk to the gate where a man let us in.

I always knew I was a pest because while I kept asking to see the barn and the cows, all I could see was the steel fence on the windows and Smiley and Mom laughing. For hours and hours we all sat in this big cafeteria room. Now and then Smiley pointed to the window and yelled, "There, there, you just missed it. A big cow just passed. Go watch. Go on." Then my mom always laughed and promised I'd get to milk one. But every Sunday time just ran out and Smiley said the cows were put back to pasture. Next time, they promised.

When I got older I finally got hip to what was up. When Smiley came back from Vietnam, he was the undefeated boxing champ of the armed forces. An army grunt himself, Smiley whipped the air force, the navy, the marines, and the Coast Guard. Everybody said Smiley might be near as good as Muhammad Ali himself. Smiley was the chosen one until he got home. Then he had no job and no high school diploma. He did like the other boxers: He trained in the day and worked as a bouncer at night in clubs and bars. He was paid good money to handle the bigmouths.

But the judge didn't care that Smiley was just doing his job when he caught this punk with his hand in the register. Smiley didn't mean to hit the guy so hard that he bled in his brain. Still, Smiley went to the farm, to prison, for twenty years. But he should've been my dad and not just my uncle (since my mom never remembered who got her pregnant in the first place).

Before jail, Smiley took me fishing in the Bronx River at night. He dressed in his old commando gear. He said "Fuck you" to the *no trespassing* signs and he snapped my first fishing rod in two.

"That ain't a way to fish," he said. He lit a cigar and opened a bag. He pulled out piles of Fourth of July ash cans, M-80s.

"We do it 'Nam style."

He lit the M-80s and dropped them into the water. The explosion came up in mud and muffled bubbles. Live things also came up, looking stunned. We got sunfish and carp and baby eels. All we had to do was net them into a pail. The ones that flopped around too much were stepped on or stabbed in the head with Smiley's army knife.

I was glad that Smiley was back. When I got to my building, the Davidson Crew was on my stoop, as always. They drank forties and smoked blunts and acted stupid. I realized that when I finally started community college it would be tough passing them without getting my books tossed around. They'd call me schoolboy and shit. But they were still the ones that kept an eye on the crack heads. They made sure that the street was safe for people like my mom who worked hard until it was dark.

"Anyone see my mom?" I asked. I had to tell her about Smiley and Slug. It didn't take a genius to know that what he did violated parole and my mom would be pissed that after all she'd done for him (like paying his rooming house), this was his thanks.

"Nah, nah," said Marv. "We ain't seen her but we heard about Smiley."

"What?" I said. "It's bullshit what you heard."

"What," said the Toad. "It's no shit. I saw it myself. The other day I was crossing Fordham Road and there was this crowd and Smiley standing over this guy who was like pinned on his steering wheel, his eyes closed, and his horn honking."

"So," I said.

"It was Smiley," said Toad. "I saw what happened myself. Smiley was in the middle of this street when this sucker in the car bopped his horn. This sucker told Smiley to move his black ass. And then—"

"Tell him," said Marv.

"There was this fucking hole clean through the windshield, a round, a perfect hole. The thing was, after that guy honked at Smiley, you know, Smiley walked up to the windshield and just ran his fist through it, through the fucking glass. He connected square on that sucker's jaw."

"And you saw it?" I said.

"I saw it and I still don't believe it. Smiley didn't even have a cut, not a scratch on his fucking hand. That's how fast and hard that nigger can punch—right through glass!"

I wasn't happy about this. This wasn't supposed to happen. My mom had waited too long. All those years Smiley was in 'Nam and then jail, all she wanted was to get back her little brother. Now it was supposed to be good. Smiley was making some money boxing guys in small gyms, even if he was old. I told the boys what I saw, what happened to Slug, *just a few minutes ago*. Marv said what I was thinking.

"Shit, the nigga's coming apart."

"Probably too many knots in the head. You know them jailhouse boxers," said Toad.

"Oh yeah," said Marv. "And I also know that Smiley's ass is going back to jail when them cops find out."

"Fuck the cops," said Toad. "Slug and his double-ugly brother will be strapped as soon as they can walk. Then they'll put a cap in Smiley's ass, you hear what I'm saying?"

"You better talk to Smiley. Warn him real fast," said Marv. "We'll tell your mom you had something to do for us. She'll understand. Don't worry."

I appreciated that. These guys knew the streets. They knew Slug better than me. I had to save Smiley. But if I wasn't home when it was dark, my mom would get worried. Then she'd get mad.

. . .

Everybody said it was a miracle. When the Vietnamese took Dien Tien, Smiley shared a piece of jungle with a bunch of guys. They got mutilated by land mines and mortars and torn to bits by snipers, but not Smiley. He walked out still smooth as a baby. My mom kept track of those battles, but even she didn't know how bad they were until the 1980s, when people began calling Vietnam vets heroes and people started making documentaries about places where Smiley fought. She watched these, shocked by the images of men dripping with blood. After that, she realized, it was probably the devil's work that got Smiley hurt while boxing.

At that time, there was this bad-ass marine who wanted to fight Smiley since Smiley was known as such a bad ass himself. So all the officers got together and arranged to have these two warriors pulled from the jungle by helicopter and sent to a boxing mat in Saigon. Everybody wanted a piece of the action. Betting went wild and even some people close to the president of the United States (so went the rumor) laid down their chips. If Smiley won, his commander promised, he would have a noncombat assignment, something in supply where Smiley could kick back in the afternoon, have a few beers and a prostitute.

Everything Smiley had heard turned out to be too real. This marine was a hard puncher with fast feet. He could jab with his right or left. The change-up disoriented Smiley in the opening rounds. And that's what finally got him laid out and left him walking around with double vision, vomiting like a drunk. After that, my mother said, Smiley was never right. But he kept on fighting. His officers sent him back to the jungle on the same helicopter that brought him out.

When I found Smiley, his buddies were watching and Smiley was trying to make a good show for them while betting dollars were dumped into a brown paper bag. As soon as the referee in the middle of this run-down arena clapped his hands, Smiley went back to his corner, one eye cut and already bleeding. His opponent, a young man greased like a body builder, never sat down. He poured water over his head and danced the Macarena in his corner. Then the referee clapped and the fighters met again, the young man doing a bull charge on Smiley. The two were at it immediately, exchanging body blows. They battled each other with the fury of children, not bothering to protect their faces. People hollered, thrilled that they were getting their money's worth.

But this was the first time I saw Smiley in a ring. This couldn't be his style. My mom always said Smiley was a submarine fighter. He'd go down and take punches, keeping his hands over his head. He'd crouch and stay low, sit on his thighs, almost squat. But if he came up periscope, my mom said, he came up in time to catch his enemy off guard, like a torpedo. They never saw it coming. It was something he brought from the bottom, from the dark, that hurt the fighters.

But now Smiley was dripping blood and his hands must've felt like hammers. He hardly lifted them as the other fighter worked his face, stick and jab. Luckily the referee's clap gave Smiley a break, and Smiley was back in his corner, looking done, his mouth too wide and sucking air.

Still, when Smiley looked over his shoulder and saw me and his buddies, he smirked. And it was a look I'd only seen in my mom's picture frame, in the photo he sent us from Saigon when he was young and proud in his new uniform, his rifle pointed toward the camera.

Round three, I think, and Smiley took another bull charge, which slowed him down again and got him taking blows to the back of his head. But at least this time Smiley went submarine. He was crouching and everybody was yelling in their loudest and cruelest voice: KILL THAT FUCK. RIP HIS HEART OUT!

Then Smiley did it, just like my mom said. Up periscope, from a dark place, down below the heavy punches; the young man couldn't even appreciate what happened. It was amazing to watch. "The only other fighter who could do that," someone said, "was Jack Dempsey."

Up from a crouch, Smiley's left foot began to lead while he extended his left jab. Then, at the same time, he suddenly launched a straight right, which was the amazing part—his right foot was now moving, and it was devastating. This was a fighter with both feet off the floor, landing a two-fisted punch, a smart bomb.

Fans jumped into the ring, stepping over the boxer who was on his back, eyes rolling in his head like rubber balls. Everybody helped Smiley raise his gloves over his head in victory.

Mom always said that Smiley didn't look good after a fight, but when I saw him in the locker room slumped in a chair with his trainer wrapping Smiley's fists in plastic bags filled with ice, dried blood caked down his face and chest, I understood the awful price he paid. He opened his eyes, barely, his eyelids puffy, and nothing registered. It was as if he was looking through me, as if he were asleep. Bob, the trainer, told me that Smiley put his winnings in an envelope for me. Bob said I should give the money to my mom. It was payback time.

I still found it odd that Smiley kept staring off into the distance, as if he'd lost something in the dark and he was trying to remember what it was. Bob said it was just a passing thing and he'd snap out of it. He also said that Smiley would surprise me. He'd remember everything we said, even if it looked like he was just sitting there dead.

"Ain't that true, Smiley, my boy?" said Bob. "You shake it off." He kneaded ice chips into the base of Smiley's neck.

Then I let it out, about Slug and what the Toad said, about punching out the windshield on Fordham Road, about parole violations and breaking my mom's heart. If Slug didn't kill him, my mom would.

"You have to do something," I said. "Wake up, man."

Then Bob put a foot in my ass. He kicked me in the butt.

"You joking me, nigger?" he said. "You come in here to bother my man about some stupid-ass junkie?"

"I only—" I said.

"Only nothing," said Bob. "You know who this man is? You just seen what he done? Don't you know this man walked out of the fucking jungles without a scratch. This man catches bullets. I saw the shit myself. And you think some punk, some slug, is bringing him down? Shit, this man danced through land mines. He slapped VC bombs out of the air. Shit, you piss-ass, you come in here, you got the nerve to talk to this man, this *man*! Shit, you better get out of my face before I throw you an ass whipping."

"Bob," said Smiley. His voice was weak. "It's cool."

I think Smiley winked at me.

"Take the money," he said. "I'll check you in the park."

"Stupid nigga," said Bob, pushing me out the door with the envelope in my hand.

"SNAP THE FUCKING BULLET OUT OF THE AIR. SNAP A BULLET?"

Marv was talking too loud, as if everybody on the street had to know my business. "That brotha is fucked up," he said.

"Those double-uglies don't play," said Toad. "I already heard they got some semiautomatics and they're gunning for Smiley. Word is on the ding dong."

"And I talked to Slug," said Marv. "He was by the park with wires all sticking in and out of his face. And the thing is, he said he was looking for *you*."

"For me?" I said.

"Fucking right," said Toad. "So you better listen up. If Smiley ain't getting the double uglies, you better get some heat and get them before they get you—and fast."

"Thing is," said Marv, "now you got us in this shit too. Being you part of our crew, if anything goes down, we gotta be soldiers for your ass."

"Thing is," said Toad, "we don't really wanna save your ass that much."

"But you guys got the guns?" I said.

Just like they thought. I was so stupid. Everybody fell off the stoop, laughing at me and shaking their heads. To them I was pathetic.

"You don't use any gun to kill someone," said Toad. "You need a special one, not easy to trace, unregistered and other shit gun."

What the fuck did I know?

"So, pay attention," said Marv. "Now you'll learn something."

All the blacks on the bus got off at this stop, the last one between our neighborhood and where we were going. We crossed Southern Boulevard into the Little Italy of the Bronx. Gone were the record stores screaming 2Pac rap music into the street. Gone were the Cuchi-Frito shops. Now we passed windows hung with salami and sidewalk cafés with Frank Sinatra posters and fat white guys smoking cigars outside social clubs called Italian American Knights or Italian American Alliance. Lots of clubs, I noticed.

And of course, why did the bus stop in front of these guys? I hesitated at the back door and felt Marv whispering in my ear, "Hey sometimes you gotta do what you gotta do. Move, sucker."

I didn't know Marv had friends in these parts. Before his dad left home, Marv was bused to a Catholic school around here. He said he met these Italian guys who "dug" him because he was like their favorite basketball star. He showed the white boys the moves.

Marv had the hoop dreams. Still, even Marv knew that the golden rule around here was "Nigger, don't let the sun set on your black ass." And since Bensonhurst, that was no secret even to herbs like me.

But Marv's old friend, Cookie, was connected. He always told Marv he had a good selection of guns, dumped from Las Vegas to places like this, the weapons of choice for mob hit men. Cookie's crew made sure the Knights of Italy respected them, too. On the walls outside the Italian club they sprayed their tag, the White Angels. When Marv asked for the Angels, the white guys laughed and spoke in Italian. One guy pointed down an alley while another guy started punching numbers into a cell phone. Great!

The sun was blazing and, peering into the glare, Marv went blindly down the alley. I tried to stay as close as possible to the wall, trying not to be seen. But then I realized I'd been holding it in, and my dick hurt and my balls, too. I had to take a piss.

Marv told me to keep my colored ass moving. The longer we hung out, the more risk we took of being misunderstood. Once we were in Cookie's turf, everything would be cool.

"I know what I'm doing," said Marv. "Just follow me."

But no matter how many times we read Cookie's address and looked up at the street signs, we still found ourselves in the wrong place, walking in circles. Finally, Marv asked a white guy who was out mowing a lawn. The guy read the address and gave us detailed directions. Left and right, down a staircase by the firehouse and up. Suddenly Marv was mad at me because after a few turns I forgot the details myself. Everything was my fault. The heat, the sun, the fact that I got everybody into this shit. But all I knew was I had to take a bad leak and I complained and whined about it.

"My dick hurts."

Marv pointed me to some garbage cans at the side of a private house, which had a nice rose garden out front. I pissed into a can while Marv sat on the street corner. He took off his bubble Nikes and massaged his toes. He leaned against a lamppost and closed his eyes. It felt like I peed forever. I noticed that the sky seemed immense and filled with changing clouds. It was real clear to me: If we got caught by some crazy Italians, they'd kill us for sure. So I decided that I was backing out of this shit and fast. I snuck away and hid from Marv. Soon after that, he began pacing the corner and calling my name.

I could tell he was freaked. I wasn't behind the cans anymore. Marv ran up and down the street. I saw someone watching me from a house, peeking from behind the curtains. Then I glanced up and saw Marv turn a corner, only he ran smack into a white lady.

That lady fell back on her butt, her grocery bag flying into the air, and Marv was down too. Then that lady let out a scream and Marv knew what time it was. He stood up and began collecting her groceries, apologizing like a pro. But as soon as that lady saw a group of white men come from a garage she started saying stuff like "He grabbed my bag. He knocked me."

Marv was going like, "Nah, nah. Please lady, come on, chill out, don't say that."

Another white lady suddenly opened her window and screamed.

"There's another one. I saw him. Over there. He's trying to sneak into that house, near the cans!"

One man pulled out a well-thumbed baseball bat.

"I say we teach this boy a lesson, like that Al Sharpton."

One man gave Marv a kick in the backside and Marv side-stepped a slap to the face.

"Now stand still," said a white guy. "We don't want to hurt you. We just want to teach you something."

Marv tried to talk fast.

"Come on, boys. I gotta friend around here, Cookie, man, the WA crew. I went to Saint Mary's."

"No shit," said a white guy. "Well, we've been looking for Cookie too. One of his boys stole my car. So, I guess you're a lucky fella today."

Just then that white lady in the window screamed again. She saw me trying to get myself around the corner and back to the bus. She pointed at me and I found myself being looked at by everybody, including Marv.

"Wait! Wait!" Marv yelled as I ran away from the crowd. And I don't know how I did it, but I found myself at the bus stop near that social club. I was under some trees. It was almost dark and I waited. Like a dummy, I forgot. I didn't have any bus money. And I wasn't about to walk out of this place. But finally, Marv showed up. He looked real tired and his face was marked up pretty bad.

What could I say to him? Why did he bring me here? It was his fault. He should've known better.

"It's your fault," I kept saying, and my chin began to tremble and shake. Tears rolled down my cheeks.

Marv grabbed me by the throat and said he was trying hard, real hard, to imagine what it was like being a punk like me. He wanted to bust my ass, he said. He wanted to beat me down. But he also said he wasn't stupid. If Smiley wasn't killed by now, he knew that beating me would only get him into deeper shit. I was lucky I had an uncle with a *rep*.

Marv let me go and I followed him onto the bus. I was surprised that he paid my fare, though he didn't look at me. We sat together in the empty bus, staring straight ahead. Then I did something I wished I never did, proving once and for all what I was: I laid my head in Marv's lap and said, "I can't make it. I'm too scared."

Then I felt Marv rub the back of my head. I opened his zipper. He must've known about me all along.

"Don't worry," he whispered. He was soft. "We're not done yet."

He slammed the clock.

"You better be teaching me," said Marv.

Suddenly Marv wanted to learn chess and play with Smiley and me. I told him not to hit the clock too hard. If he broke it, I'd have to tell Smiley the truth when he showed up. But I was glad Marv sat with me. With Slug on the hunt, I was afraid to be alone, especially in the park. But now that Marv was packing (he brought a gun for Smiley), I wasn't worried one bit. I was having fun.

"Let me show you the faux pas," I told Marv, taking his horse with my pawn.

"You shitting me?" he said. "A pawn can do that?"

"It can," I said. "Now I'm teaching you. I like that."

"Well, I don't like that move," said Marv, knocking my pawn off the board. Just then, cutting through the park from the avenue, moving too fast for anything good, I saw my mom.

"She's crying," I said.

Marv slipped his hand under my shirt and put his gun to my ribs.

"You know nothing," he said. "Now *I'm* looking out for you, remember."

My Protector

Was that him? It couldn't—

He did the same old pimp roll down the Great White Way, wearing his flak jacket and motorcycle boots. Most people stepped out of his way—and fast. Those who didn't got the elbow. He fought the crowds on Times Square. The old killing machine, ex-marine, bopped his way straight into the Circus to find some porno queens, no doubt.

At least that's what I thought. . . .

But I wasn't about to cross the street to find out. I was glad he didn't see me in the shadows of the bookstore even though my Mercedes was double-parked, and I ran the risk of being towed.

But why the hell did they let him out? What kind of prison system was this?

When I got home I made a few phone calls. I couldn't believe that anybody in this city was stupid enough to give him probation. Not with his record: robbery, grand theft auto, not to mention murder. I thought he had twenty-five years to life!

. . .

"How could they let him out?" I yelled into the phone. That brought Keisha, my wife, out of the kitchen.

"What's all the yelling about?"

"Nothing!" I slammed the receiver down on the phone. I cut past Keisha on my way to the liquor cabinet. I poured a shot of scotch.

"Nothing?" Keisha grabbed the glass before it wet my lips.

"You don't drink," she said.

"That was before."

I grabbed my scotch and Keisha waited.

"So?" she said.

I gulped the drink. Maybe I was overreacting, but I wanted her to understand the seriousness of the situation. Danyel was out and I didn't know when he'd show up on my doorstep. Not to mention my office. I pictured myself sneaking out the back door with Danyel in hot pursuit. Prison didn't build men, it destroyed them, and Danyel . . .

In the fourteen years I'd known him, he had always been in trouble. He was always in the principal's office. He stole chocolate milk from kids and terrorized teachers with spit balls. Sometimes he tore their textbooks or stole their cars from the school parking lot.

"So I'm sorry," I told my wife. "We leave town, tonight."

"Be serious," she said. "He's out. Big deal. You didn't have a hand in any murder, did you?"

"No, no," I said. "You're right. I didn't do anything. It's not that serious. It's only *very* serious."

And it was. I wasn't lying. . . .

Even though Danyel and I weren't great friends, he was always my protector, and I needed one. We were kids living in the South Bronx. That meant we lived with crews like the Savage Skulls and the Reapers, and they didn't let us forget it. Sometimes these gangs jumped us and stole our money and our coats and new shoes. So Danyel and me stuck together. We weren't just little kids. We were different.

Danyel was muscular and I was flabby. Danyel studied judo and I didn't. Danyel carried a pocket knife and I read chess books. In fact, kids on my block called me a faggot. They asked me for blow jobs and pinched my breasts, which were fat. Then they tweaked my nipples and laughed. Yet Danyel told them all that I was his boy. He stood up for me. He had a knife and he'd use it, too.

Danyel came from a tough family, and I didn't. His father came home drunk in the middle of the night and beat him until someone called the cops. So Danyel said he wasn't afraid to fight anyone. He'd done it with his old man, his whole life.

But I was afraid. Unlike Danyel's father, mine came from a small southern town where they put more faith in divine retribution than in earthly punishment. If I did something wrong, I was quickly reminded: Sooner or later I'd have to answer for it at the pearly gates.

My father actually believed in the golden rule: "Do unto others as you would have others do unto you." Which all sounded fine and dandy in some Bible class, but on my block the kids had another rule, the rule of the street: FUCK THEM, BEFORE THEY FUCK YOU. So my father couldn't give me what I needed to survive, like a good knife and kick-boxing lessons.

Danyel, on the other hand, was always on the street looking after me, even if my Dad didn't like us hanging together. I did it anyway. And I was grateful. Danyel saved my ass more than once, which is why he ended up in jail.

It all started as one of those usual shakedowns. Bogie, the president of the Turbans, the toughest gang on our street, decided he was teaching me a lesson. He said his girlfriend had a crush on me. He said I was flirting with her. I think I saw that girl like once in my school yard and I said hello. She said I was real cute, like a fat little puppy. But I didn't like her. Still, Bogie said he wasn't about to let his woman get her "pussy wet" with some punk—not even in her dreams.

At least that's what Bogie said. And I would've been dead if Bogie hadn't made a big mistake. He put the word on the ding-dong that he was looking for me. Danyel got a whiff of it and secretly followed Bogie around a corner, carrying a lead pipe.

I didn't know anything about it. I was on my stoop reading a book when Bogie came up on me and accused me of messing with his bitch. I tried to talk my way out of it without getting myself stomped into a pool of blood. I didn't have a reputation to protect, like Danyel. So I cringed and begged Bogie to let me go. That is when Danyel appeared from behind a wall. He laid that pipe across Bogie's skull with a crack.

That was the last time I saw him. Danyel was arrested and Bogie nearly dead. Yet the judge took pity on Danyel. Since he was young (and Bogie was a thug himself), the judge gave Danyel a choice: Go to Riker's Island or join the marines. Danyel decided to serve his country.

But most of the time Danyel was in the brig. He didn't see the world. Instead he was discharged, dishonorably, and so he hit the streets with a vengeance. He wore a green beret and said he could rip out a person's heart. He was now a professional, a trained government killer. But without an education, he wasn't exactly employable. He turned to robbing cabs with a gun, which is how he ended up in jail. He shot a driver for ten bucks, a twenty-two-year-old college student.

Shot him in the chest and left him to bleed to death, slumped over a steering wheel on a quiet street.

So why the hell did they let him out?

After a few days, I finally got tired of looking over my shoulder, waiting for Danyel to appear. My wife was right. New York was a big city; people got lost all the time. He'd never find me. I wanted to believe it. I even called the Department of Corrections. They said they had an eye on him. They assured me that he was reporting to his probation officer on schedule. If he farted the wrong way, they swore, he'd be back in jail in a minute.

"I told you, you silly," my wife said, grinning ear to ear.

"I am a silly," I said.

Since I saw Danyel, I'd stopped jogging in the park, afraid he'd be waiting for me in the bushes. I even canceled business appointments, which cost me money. I'd gone into mortgage banking. But on this glorious Sunday morning, my wife encouraged me to live. Live life again.

And live I would. I put on my sweat suit and promised to return with the bagels and *The New York Times*.

I felt great, which is why I was so baffled when I saw my building lobby. It was littered with crushed beer cans and strewn with broken glass. Someone had also ripped out the doorbells. The metal wall panel dangled from a gaping black hole, the wires hanging out.

Danyel was back.

I ran up my stairs two at a time and double-locked the door behind me. I should've listened to my father. He was right. Hanging out with guys like Danyel had its price. After Bogie's attack, I was suspended from school. The principal figured birds of a feather flocked together blah, blah, blah. He was tired of Turbans haunting his hallways looking for me. Besides, I could hardly go to class anyway, knowing that they were out there, and my father never forgave me. Since it was poverty that kept us there, my father had to go to the Housing Authority, as well as the Welfare Department, to see social workers and beg for money to help us move. We were prisoners.

There was a housing shortage, a crisis. It was all my fault. Finally, someone in a city agency listened to my dad's cry for help. We moved to the North Bronx, a housing project. Yet I didn't ask Danyel to use a lead pipe on Bogie, did I? It wasn't my fault that Danyel spent the best years of his life behind bars while I went to a community college to become a small-business man, and I married a woman who grew up with money on Harlem's Sugar Hill.

Still, I could already feel Danyel disapproving of all I'd worked for:

my new condo, my fancy car. I could already see him standing on my Swedish rug, surrounded by my potted plants. He'd only see the things he could've had if it weren't for me. I imagined him in a rage, running through my apartment with his pipe, clobbering everything in sight. Then he'd clobber me.

That night, I slept with a light on—when I did sleep. The probation office was running a check on Danyel. They said they'd call me in an emergency. I was already in bed when the phone rang.

"Pick up," said my wife.

"It could be him," I said.

"What if it's the probation officer?"

"At this hour?" I said. "It's after midnight."

I let the phone ring.

"Maybe they caught him," said Keisha. "Come on. He destroyed our lobby."

I picked up the phone. It was him.

"Danyel . . . hey, no kidding. . . . Out, huh."

My wife sat up and stared at me, raising her "what's up" eyebrows.

"Yeah, well, I'll have to ask my wife . . . yeah, married. . . . He'd like to come by for a drink."

My wife shrugged.

"Okay, yeah, sure. Why not? Uh-huh. See you then, homeboy."

I hung up.

"You invited him?" my wife said, alarmed, looking scared.

"It was him. What could I say?"

"For Christ's sake!" My wife grabbed the phone and dialed. "We'd better tell someone."

"Why? He hasn't done anything—anything we could prove. Anyone could've attacked the lobby. The neighborhood kids."

"But do we have to see him?"

Danyel was paying me back, shutting me in. I was angry. I even resented my wife.

The next day, she set out a fancy spread: turkey julienne, cheese, and smoked salmon.

"For God's sake," I said. "Don't overdo it. He's a murderer."

"What's bugging you? If they let him out, he can't be that bad. Besides, it was your idea."

"Yeah, but look at you."

She wore her leather pumps, string of pearls, business suit, and she had put fresh flowers in a designer vase.

"So, murderer or not, he was your friend, your protector, wasn't he?"

Maybe that was it. I also had put on a suit and I'd even shaved. But when I looked around my apartment, everything seemed to slap me in the face. Danyel went to jail and I didn't. I had things and he didn't.

Damn him!

There was a knock on the door. I wanted to climb down my fire escape and run out the back alley.

"I'll get it," my wife said.

I followed behind. It was him. He wore his old bomber jacket. He had a mustache and a scar on the nose. That was new.

"Keisha, I'm Terry's wife. Nice to meet you."

She offered Danyel her hand, but he ignored it and looked at me.

"Terr," he said, as if he couldn't believe it was really me.

"Danyel," I said. "So, can I get you something? A drink?"

Danyel glared at the spread on the dining room table. My wife put out a silver cheese slicer and crystal wineglasses.

"Would you like pâté?" she asked.

"Say what?" Danyel turned on her. "What kind of shit you handing me? Looks like dog vomit."

Why'd I let him in? He was in my house and he was taking over. I should've known better. He can't push us around. I should say something, but I was never a fighter. I looked at the cheese slicer; and if push came to shove, I wondered if I'd use it. FUCK THEM BEFORE THEY FUCK YOU.

He'd insulted me; he'd dissed my wife, hadn't he? I began looking at the door, hoping some cops would burst in to save us. But it was locked and Danyel kept taking in the apartment.

"So, you makin' out, huh?"

"Well—"

Before I could answer, Danyel was in a rage. He turned on me: I was a goddamn pussy, he said, an ass-wipe. That's right. I ran out on him. I was a punk. He wrote letters and I never wrote back. And wasn't he my protector? Wasn't he always there for me? How could I abandon him?

"I don't know," I said, not knowing how to respond. Danyel grabbed the cheese slicer.

"How much did this cost ya?"

"I don't remember," I said.

Danyel crossed the room and opened my liquor cabinet. He grabbed a bottle of vodka. Suddenly he stuck the cheese slicer into his back pocket. Then he dropped into an armchair.

"Look," my wife said, breaking the silence, "if you need a little money, you don't have to take the slicer. It was my mom's."

"That so?" said Danyel, grinning.

"Keisha," I said. "Forget it."

I knew the game. It was street justice. He had us where he wanted us. He had the slicer and we were the assholes. Street justice. He drank straight from my bottle, guzzled the vodka until it spilled from his mouth and down his chest, staining the rug. He burped. Street justice.

"You know who fucked up your hall, don't you?" he said.

"I can figure it out," I said. "I grew up in the South Bronx, remember? So let's cut the shit. What do you really want?"

"Excuse me?" Danyel said. "You're not threatening me, are you, nigger? In jail, I'd sell your asshole by the hour."

He put down the bottle, got up, and walked toward me. We were toe-to-toe.

"Maybe we should eat," said Keisha.

"Skip it," said Danyel. "I got a date. I'm going to the Circus."

"Oh," said Keisha, "I didn't know the circus was in town."

Danyel smirked, self-satisfied. He handed me the vodka. Then he took the slicer from his pocket and laid it on the salmon. He moved to the door.

"But don't you worry," he said. "I'll be seeing you."

He was gone, slamming the door behind him instead of my head.

My wife turned the lock.

"Call the police," she said.

"Shhh," I said at the peephole. "He might be listening."

"What do we do?"

"Where's the paper?" I whispered. "Give me the newspaper."

"Why?" my wife said, handing me *The New York Times.*

"I'll tell you why," I said. I grabbed the paper and turned to the real estate section—New Jersey. "We're moving."

Gangsta Bond

"Yo, your bitch save some G?" The young drug lord with a big future was telling me like it is: "You think you're real dope now, living it up with your income, but one day you'll end up in the street collecting soda cans."

"So," I asked, "what am I supposed to do?"

"Man, it's easy. Make some investments, sit back and let the interest kick in."

Great. I'd heard that one before. That was Great Idea number 999. I already tried that at the beginning of my career as a gangsta rapper. One month before I married Mermaid, I went to her drug king for some advice on what to do with my new wealth.

It was $10,000 at the time, an advance on my first album, *High & Rising*. But Mermaid knew how I tore through cash, so she made me save before it was too late.

"Now," this drug king had said, "you don't want government bonds. They're too easy to cash. Besides, you don't want them feds knowing what you got. Those assholes will tax your interest—word to the mother!"

He suggested his personal investment package, which was guaranteed (on a handshake) to double, triple, and quadruple my money in an unspecified amount of time. And so on that day my new career of putting together capital began. On that day, it ended too.

Mermaid and me married in the South Bronx, when prices for everything in New York City were higher than they'd ever been in the history of the universe. I had just gotten my second advance on my new album so I was feeling like, "Yo, kiss my butt" to all them millionaires I'd seen driving down Fifth Avenue in their limos. Like, my income just doubled itself in thirty days.

It'd done this for the first few months after my record hit the stands. Straight up! So I was sure this was going to last forever. I was just waiting for my first million; and like, given the situation, saving seemed like a big waste of time—hear what I'm saying?

Mermaid and me got fired up. We rented an apartment in one of the most expensive hotels in the world, the Plaza. And both of us just had to buy ourselves matching $20,000 lynx coats. We just had to use the new Visa Gold to go with the gold-labeled breakfast champagne—*you know what I'm saying?*

Now boo-yaa, we weren't planning on dying or nothing in that hotel suite. We just figured it was a fly place to hang until we had enough G to take a trip overseas. SEE THE WORLD, SUCKERS. I already had my own show on *Yo MTV Raps: Get Set V.O.P.* (Voice of the Projects). I was kicking it, as they say in show biz. I was Chilly P. and I was chillin'.

But to make my long story short: After being married for like a year, I woke up one day to find that I didn't have a penny to my name. And the bill at the Plaza was five months overdue, like fifty G.

I will never forget that sick, lame-to-the-wood feeling I got when I left my bank.

"Whassup?" Mermaid asked. I joined her on the sidewalk. "You look like you been *dissed*."

"Not that," I said all happy like. "I'm just a little fucking surprised to find out that we ain't got any money left."

"No money?" she calmly repeated as we began to walk toward Harlem like we was in a trance.

"Well," she said, "how about a movie?"

It was all so calm. The bank manager hadn't even looked me in the eye. I'd walked in and asked, "How much I got?"

He punched my bank code. "None."

That was it. There was no cursing on my part, no eye jamming. Fuckit. I figured there was nothing to worry about. Wasn't I a famous rap artist? *Get Set V.O.P.* All I had to do was sign some checks. How could I be poor? Being poor meant living back in the hood, ducking drive-bys and being depressed. But wasn't I living in the most expensive place in the galaxy?

My first step, naturally, was to try and collect on my only asset, my $10,000 investment sealed on a handshake with Mermaid's drug buddy. But then Mermaid stopped me. She got all choked up, saying the investment was like some family heirloom. "It's our bond," she said, throwing herself on the bed, weeping her head off. So instead of a movie, I got myself booked on the *Yo! Raps Game Show* hosted by M. C. Mike. That night, I studied with Mermaid. She read me the answers and I had to tell her the questions. She pretended she was M. C. Mike.

Me: Okay, M.C., for five hundred bucks, I'll take number two across.
M.C.: *Flashdance*, featuring the Rock Steady Crew.
Me: What was the first film to show the world b-boying [break dancing]?
M.C.: That is absolutely correct. Now would you like to go for a thousand?
Me: Yes, M.C. Give me double or nothing on number seven down.

M.C.: "La Di-Da-Di" by Doug E. Fresh and Slick Rick.
Me: I gotta think a minute, M.C.
M.C.: All you got is a minute, Chilly P.
Me: I think . . . speaking of expletives, upon which hip-hop recording do the words *bitch* and *pussy* both appear for the very first time?
M.C.: Give the man a big hand! Give him the bonus round.

Mermaid and me went to bed that night, our hearts steaming with hope. And the very next morning, our money crisis was over. My agent said that with such a hot rapper like myself, record companies were eager to advance on future royalties. (They hoped I was working on a second album.) And so I learned a valuable lesson that day, and that was: Money just had a way of turning up when I needed it the most. If things got really bad, yo, I could now borrow.

But for the first three years of my marriage, my income just improved, steadily averaging around $90,000 every ten months. So we indulged ourselves like with a baby and a trip to Africa. All that time, money just seemed to come to me easier and easier with less and less effort. My music was turning up in Nike commercials, Speedo and McDonald's.

With a little more time, I even felt like it was possible to save. So we left the Plaza and bought into a Park Avenue brownstone for $5,000 a month. We hired a full-time baby-sitter for $1,800 a month and her husband at $2,000. We needed a building manager since I didn't know shoop about boilers and pipes. There was also the cook at $1,000 and my driver. So, basically, we told ourselves that I was going to earn about $160,000 that year and we were going to live on $25,000, leaving at least $5,000 with which to buy ourselves some security for old age.

Truth was, *Get Set V.O.P.* was canceled. My record sales were slumping. Word on the street was (word in the music rags, the *Rap Sheet* was) I was living large and living with them rich white folks. They even had pictures of me and Mermaid popping out of lime-colored limos like we was Prince Charles and Lady Di. "Problem is," my agent said, "the gangsta M.C. needs the ghetto to justify his every rhyme. Without that, you fall off, you become a tired studio rapper. Gangstas got to convince the audience that his shit is real!"

"But damn," I told my agent. "What's with the double standard? No Eddie Murphy, Bill Cosby, Michael Jordan, or Arsenio Hall ever moved onto my block when I was in the South Bronx. I never seen them moving back to the ghetto. No Richard Pryor. And look at that loudmouth Spike Lee. He's always running off on how rich brothers got to get together and do something for the people. Like, I studied film at Bronx Community College (it was that, said the judge, or jail, grand theft auto). I never saw Spike Lee. That nigga was too busy teaching white boys at Yale or someplace like that. But of course, he did do something for the people. He opened the Joint, Spike's place to sell the brothers his line of All-Star b-boy caps at bullshit prices—prices he knows will make some who can't afford it (but they just got to have it) kill for it. Motherfuckers already shoot each other for too-expensive Nikes."

"Hey, hey, forget Spike and all that," said my agent. "The real issue is—and I warned you years ago—that one day the record companies would find gangsta rap too hot to handle. You already got Time Warner looking to sell their rap labels, but no one is buying. Problem is, people just started listening real close to the music and they're saying, Black people too, 'I don't want my kids singing this shit.' "

In case I forgot, my agent read me some lyrics from my first hit single:

Take her, and bug her
Turn her, and tug her
And if she mumbles
Bang her boy,
Bang her again.

Give her cold jelly
To take in her belly
And if she stands all the pain
Then knock out her brains.

I had to admit, those days were hard core. I was young. But now that I had a kid, even I began to wonder, could I end up in the street collecting soda cans? So I decided, like everybody knows: When you *really* want to save, you need to buy yourself a book and print your name on the front in big letters. You need a budget book to write down every bill that comes into the house. That way, you could at least watch the everyday spending and hack away at it until it's nothing.

But then again, now that Mermaid and me were part of this new rich class, we got the feeling that all them magazines that told wealthy folks what to buy were actually focused right on us. Now when I say rich, you probably imagine some fat guy who got himself a face-lift and a sixteen-year-old girlfriend. But I can testify, knowing some rich folks, this picture is totally off.

I'm hardly a used-up man at twenty-three years old, and most of my friends, the rap stars, are younger than me. And many of them got more money than all them big-butt executives, tax lawyers, and college-boy record producers. And I'm saying this because what most people don't know is that the ghetto is set up—it's prepared to keep money moving all the time, 24/7, day and night. The drugstore never closes. Why do you think them Koreans are doing the lobster bit?

So when I opened my store (not far from Spike's), I had a neon sign, *GET SET V.O.P.* I sold my own line of b-boy caps, around the clock. And I'm talking about eleven-year-old kids coming in with pockets bulging with bills, bringing down $100 a day for just watching a street corner, for whistling when the heat was up. It wasn't long before my block saw the grand opening of two major fast-food chains, not to mention one of them Pathmark SuperStores that looked like it was just sucked right off the hide of a suburban mall. They know where the cash flows.

The problem was, naturally, people started rushing to these superstores for them super prices. Pathmark even ran its own line of b-boy caps that looked a lot like mine (and Spike's) at half the price. It quickly became clear: It was now impossible for all of us to live off the same street. So each of us just waited for the other sucker to give up and move out. I was already slashing my prices left and right.

But despite the growing bills (and my failing business), Mermaid and me began the year with high hopes. My new album promised to be hot at the record store and even if living in a brownstone drove up expenses (it had a leaky roof, and bad wiring), a film deal suddenly seemed possible. And I figured that would easily take up the difference. My agent said, "You might see gigantic sums at the box office." Just to be sure, I called a rapper I knew in L.A. to get the maximums and the minimums. I didn't want to be unreasonable, so I planned on a figure somewhere in the middle, and I told Mermaid we could count on that as income. So we wrote it in our book and spent it like we had it. I believe the figure was around $260,000.

It was a great year. *Tired Ass Nigga*, my new album, was a flop. But no matter! We always had that movie deal to look forward to. The producers projected at least a $10 million b.o. on the film's opening weekend. We would finally pay off our brownstone. And saving would be so easy we would do it blindfolded, sitting on a park bench with our hands tied behind our backs.

In fact, like a good omen, we began that summer with a piece of good luck from an unexpected source. A computer company wanted to do a CD-ROM thing with my music.

For the first time, we had a little extra to buy our first real investment, a tax-free bond from a bank. It was a very exciting experience for me, the signing of the papers under the watchful gaze of an armed security guard. Then the bank manager and me descended a silver staircase that led to a more impressive steel vault that was under the manager's personal direction. There I was handed a brass key to open my safe-deposit box to protect my $50,000 note, my bond.

I left the bank feeling real solid and fresh. I was finally launching a career in collecting capital. "Hell," the bank manager said, "if you die today, if you are killed, your wife would already get at least $3,000 a year in interest alone, as long as she lived."

"That," I announced at dinner, "is what I call providing for my family." Mermaid looked satisfied. The next step was basically getting that box office money into the same bank account. In fact, from that day on, I worried less and less about our expenses. If we dropped a few thousand here or there, so what? If our food bills varied mysteriously from month to month, why worry? If I hired an MBA to run my store, if I overstocked b-boy caps, what the fuck? I even bought and sold Spike Lee shirts at ridiculously low prices. I had a bond in the bank, didn't I?

True, the coupons were sent directly to my agent, so I didn't exactly have the pleasure of clipping them myself. But I knew everything was secure in my file in my agent's office—even though I had to dispose of some bonds just two months after I locked them in the vault. Fact is, I began work on another album and it seemed like a good idea to live off the bonds until I finished the recording. But everything was moving slower than planned. So coupons had to be clipped at a faster and faster pace.

But the movie was opening in a few months, and to hold us over Mermaid suggested I go back to the clubs, to do a live performance for easy quick bucks. "But then I'll never finish my record," I complained. I was sure this one was really in line with rap's new direction. I was doing love songs, raps for Valentine's Day. I even cut a deal with Raffi to do some kid songs, "Smokey Pokey" in rap. There was no need to work. I took the borrowing road like we'd done before. (My new record company didn't have the cash to do an advance.)

So, I went back to Mermaid's drug-dealing pal, who still held that $10,000 investment, the family heirloom. He agreed to make me an advance against my future earnings (on the handshake).

Then on Christmas, the film (*Gangsta Fairyland*) opened in Hollywood. There was a tremendous chill. People rustled their popcorn bags and coughed out loud. Some left their seats as if to go to the bathroom but never returned. Even I left after thirty minutes. I wanted to blow up the movie projector myself. It was the shitty script. I looked good on the screen and I felt my music was dope in surround sound.

After a bad week of harassing the movie people, looking for my money, my agent finally convinced me to give up and come home.

But I couldn't believe that my first great year had ended so fast. I was $160,000 in debt and my newest Great Idea was to get in touch with a homeless shelter that had a room with hot water for nothing a week. "But at least," I told Mermaid, "we spent enough, we sure bought us the right to call ourselves the new rich. What more could money buy?"

So my first next step was to shut down V.O.P., a.s.a.p. Then I went straight to the vault. The manager assured me the bond still had some value. But she promised if I was overdrawn on my checking one more time, she'd shut me down.

"And no," she said, "I never go out for drinks with my depositors." She considered rap musicians a shiftless bunch, and she reminded me that the bank was burglar proof cellar to ceiling.

I was too angry to put the bond back into the vault. I shoved it into my pocket and took the subway home. I was ruined, my connections drained. I decided then and there to make a list of all that Mermaid and me could sell (like in an auction, which sounds classy):

CD players
Computers, printers
Microwave ovens
TV sets

A clay ashtray made by a convict who used to be a famous rap star
A $10,000 investment held on a handshake by a promising drug czar

"Now," I said, "let's really cut the shit out of our expenses."

Mermaid was right with me. She said there was a grocery store where if you used cash everything was half price. "Cash!" I laughed. "It's too late for cash! We ain't got any. So you just go down to that store and get down on your knees and beg for credit."

"Well then," said Mermaid, "we just let go of the maid, the cook, and the building manager. They got to go."

"Go?" I said. "You can't just let people go. They need severance pay, and two weeks' notice. You don't turn off a person's paycheck—toss people into the street. Besides, if we really sink, we'll need them to go down to the Bowery to stand on line for us at the soup kitchen."

"Well," said Mermaid, "then we have to budget."

"We can't," I said. "We're too poor to economize. It's too late. The only way to go now is extravagance."

"Why don't we give up the house? Get a studio?"

"Impossible. Moving costs too much money. And we'd have to pay for storage for all the shit we can't sell. And worse, with all the confusion of moving, I couldn't focus on my music, which is the only way I know to get us out of this mess."

There was a bare room in my basement. I sat there all night with my electric heater at my feet (no money for oil). The next day I emerged with new songs, which I managed to sell to some hot rap stars I knew. At least I could make a few mortgage payments and cover some outstanding bills.

It took twelve hours a day for two months to get almost out of poverty. But not enough rappers took my stuff and those that did never recorded it. And I really wasn't happy about what had happened. How had we spent nearly $200,000? Two hundred thousand dollars wasn't that rich. We didn't own a yacht or a Michael Jackson mansion. What had $200,000 really gotten us? My roof still had a leak.

I dug up Mermaid's budget book. The complete household record. I found trips, concert tickets, sports events, garden costs, restaurants, movies, my kid's expenses, the help. "Not so bad," I said, adding it up. But then Mermaid handed me the items marked *pleasure*:

Gambling
Partying

Gifts
Bar bills

I added it up. "Great," I said. "Just under twenty thousand a month. At least now we know where to cut back. We know where the money went." But Mermaid stared at the figures, confused.

"What's wrong?"

"It's not the items," she said. "It's the total. You got twenty thousand but the bank says we spent twenty-eight thousand a month last year. Are you saying we lost ninety-six thousand dollars?"

"Give me a pencil," I said.

For over two hours we worked and reworked the numbers in silence. "No change."

"That's impossible!" I screamed. "You don't just lose track of ninety-six thousand dollars."

"It's just not here."

Then there was a knock at the door. I answered it, still dazed by the figures in my head. It was the Rockpools, our lawyer friends, our neighbors from England.

"We just lost ninety-six thousand dollars."

"Thieves," said Mrs. Rockpool, looking around nervously. We

explained the situation, how this money mysteriously disappeared, vanished into thin air.

"Well," said Mrs. Rockpool, "what we have is a budget."

"Yes, we have a budget," Mr. Rockpool agreed. "And we stick to it even if the heavens fall. We don't go over it. That's the only way to live."

"Then that's what we must do," I said. "Have a budget and stick to it. Everybody with brains does it."

"Yes," said Mr. Rockpool, filling his glass with my expensive gin. "I pity anybody that doesn't have a system."

"How much have you saved so far?" Mermaid asked.

"So far?" said Mrs. Rockpool. "So far we haven't saved anything. We only just developed our system yesterday."

"Yesterday!" I cried out.

"Just yesterday, dear fellow," said Mr. Rockpool. "But I wish to God I started it years ago. I went over my accounts and I still can't find eighteen thousand dollars to save my soul."

So, at least our troubles were over. We left the newly rich set forever and installed a real budget. It's actually such a simple system I could tell it to you in a few words. You slice up your income into a big pizza pie with each slice standing for a different expense. In fact, we got the pie on CD-ROM so the computer does all the work for you. Now you know exactly what part of your earnings you can spend on each slice. For example, I can see that the amount to spend on movie tickets should be one-eight of our medical bills. This allows us to see one movie every six months. And since we moved back into the projects with Mermaid's mom, we don't even have the rent to pay. That leaves us a little cash to spend on magazine ads to revive my public image now that them magazines killed off my rap career: Chilly P. is DOA. And if the promises made by the new computer system are correct, if I ever make money again, we might even save $5,000.

Still, I couldn't get my hands on that missing $96,000. "If only we had something to show for it," I yelled at my wife. "I feel like such a chump." Even the family heirloom, "our bond," was gone, killed by a rival in a drive-by.

"Dumb, dumb," I said.

My wife looked at me and thought long and hard. Finally, she said, "I know what you should do. Why don't you write a story about a gangsta star, like you, who loses all his money. I bet they pay for it. Could even make a movie."

"That," I replied coldly, "is the stupidest, the dumbest, idea I ever heard."

The Male Bond

I may have character. I learned that the other day sitting with my pal M.B. We each had an elephant's ear and a cup of latte macchiato. We sat under a green awning at a sidewalk café in Greenwich Village. The sky blackened, the wind blew, and a hard rain came down mixed with hail. M.B. said something with a literary flair about the white hail / the black sky. He couldn't help himself. His name had just appeared in the *Best Stories of 1994* at the back of the fat yellow book. He was listed among the 100 distinguished writers. In other words, you could read his name but not his story.

I don't recall what he said exactly, but it was what you'd expect from one of the best, and it was said loud enough to get the waitress's attention just as she was leaning her body between us, over the white tablecloth, to press a button that lowered the awning to keep us dry.

Then she took our empty cups. M.B. said she was cute. She had black hair, black boots, a black Danskin, and black lace stockings torn at the knees. She was punk pale with thick red lips. At this point, I wanted to respond to M.B. in a number of ways. I wanted to add my own literary allusion to the hail. And I was quite excited about it (though I don't sound like it now). I also wanted to comment on the cuteness of the waitress to fulfill a male bonding opportunity—given that we're balding, over-forty guys with intelligent wives and a daughter each.

We're cool guys, too, cool enough to be publicly "feminized" and privately horny—horny enough to comment on the waitress's boobs, cold and nippled, stretched between us over the white tablecloth during the freezing hail. In fact, M.B. later said (close to my ear), "I'd like to take lipstick. Put a 'W' on either side of her ass; a 'W' on the right cheek and a 'W' on the left. Then I'd like to spread her apart and go WOW!"

"Yes," I added. "But if you turned her upside down, and spread her ass again, she'd spell MOM."

Sexist, horny pigs (privately). But our wives were publicly sexist and privately "feminized." They liked to comment on the tight buns of waiters, and on men with graying temples and beautiful eyes.

They fully enjoyed the new Coke commercial: a group of women, secretaries and executives alike, rush to a window and leer at the pecs of a construction worker who strips off his shirt. But if you accuse them of sexism, they'll say you just don't get it. Two wrongs don't make a right. They make it even.

But we're cool enough to know—PC enough—we'd better not

leer at the great "bods." After all, unlike other men who spend their lives among adults, we're among the young, the radical, and the feminist. Thus we wear contemporary modes of clothing and mimic contemporary modes of speech. We listen to everything from NWA (Niggas with Attitude) and liberally quote their work (our other male bond): "Fuck the police, comin' straight from the underground. A young nigga got it bad."

We're college teachers of the worst kind, creative writers who revel in eccentricity, each of us sporting an earring, the silver studs. We give the young something to aspire to, and we've agreed, despite the male bonding opportunity, we won't fuck the waitress—if we could. We are impressed by our self-restraint. After twenty years of marriage, neither of us has taken advantage of the girls in our classes, their jeans, slim legs spread before us. (Surely, in the shower, each of us has rubbed our own mushroom raw imagining the possibilities in our offices; jaws locked, and the doors too.) We patted each other on the back, did the high five and hugged. Our restraint awed us, though we couldn't keep our eyes off the cold nipples, now budded and taut under the waitress's shirt, rubbed and polished red each time she bent over to refill our cups.

But this restraint is actually another literary allusion I wanted to share with M.B. Writers each, we are sensitive to contemporary modes of speech, and so I've noticed that often, by our own admission, we are not what we seem. The truth is:

We teach writing at a community college. Our students come from New York City's "ethnic" neighborhoods, like Howard Beach and Bensonhurst. The girls before us do not have their legs spread, their loins pulsing for us. They wear gold virgins around their necks and blow gum through their front teeth. They call each other "princess" and imitate Andrew Dice Clay, a so-called comedian, a stand-up who does nursery rhymes about niggers with big lips. The girls snap their fingers to it—but it's not all of them. It's just some of them who make it feel like all, which is the problem with literary allusion. (Black sky / white hail. White waitress / black panties.)

The allusion just builds and builds, and before you know it you have all allusion and no story: women with their legs spread (white) and pubes exposed (black), when in fact they don't.

"But story is character," says M.B., one of the Best of 1994, since we've been discussing our favorite thing, creative writing.

But I don't want to go back and change this, which may be the difference between M.B. and me. I'm at this point now: I'm too old to do the crap I foist on my students: setting tone, place, climax, and anticlimax. I'm too old to spend time on this stuff. One publication, more or less, won't alter my life. I have tenure, so fuck it. Even M.B.

can't hide from the fact that at his age one's name on a list of 100 does not make a star.

Still, M.B. is determined to give me his advice on how to improve my writing so I too can see my name (and not my story) in the back of the fat yellow book. I feign interest (not willing to forgo this potential male bonding moment). And then I realize that M.B. is speaking in a voice too loud. I notice the waitress is ignoring her customers. But instead of getting to the point, M.B. is prattling on about his Katherine Anne Porter Prize. He repeats the prize's name (*as if I need reminding*). I edited drafts of that story long before our silver studs were put in.

But then again, I must shamefully admit, I found myself equally loud and repetitious, alluding now to my role as number one reader on the prize story to convey to you-know-who that I too was a creative force to be reckoned with. (The cold nipple, polished and red / the mushrooms, the heads rubbed raw.) I'm the master of literary allusion. There are secrets here, right now, which I could exploit if I only went back and changed this.

Still, M.B. got the prize and I didn't. He ignored my advice, and so now I ignore his. The waitress seems a better way to keep things interesting. Her body stretched between us . . . his hand on her right breast, my hand on the left; his tongue buried in her right ear, mine in the left; two elephant ears, two holes, two men, the coffee cups rattling between us, spilling and staining the white tablecloth black. (The black sky / the white hail. The white skin/the black clothes. The white legs / the black pubes.)

"But it's character," M.B. keeps insisting. "That's the key." His philosophy (the Best of 1994) is: Always put characters in situations where they must act in ways that go against their character (i.e., the priest kills). He says it's called paradox.

M.B. grew up in James Baldwin's neighborhood and went to Baldwin's high school. There M.B. was a star, the boy who graduated high school at sixteen and found himself a freshman at Berkeley in California. There, he claims, he began his days as a student dissident, his days as the campus SDS organizer, his days storming the ROTC office, burning draft cards, and marching on Washington to Free the Chicago Seven, Free Huey, Free the Black Panthers, Free Angela, Free Manson, Free Ho Chi Minh, and Free Love.

He did it all, he said, Power to the People, and ended up in a federal prison, a political voice to be feared in the land of the free.

Only one day he left me alone in his wife's art studio where he kept a steamer trunk too big for his actual living space (a Thompson Street railroad flat with a claw foot bathtub still in the kitchen next to the grease-splattered stove, which looked old enough to burn timber). Big Mistake. Be a person on whom nothing is lost. Be a writer. Somewhere I heard that, and it's long been on my computer bubble quiz, which is laser scanned and automatically graded.

I opened the trunk and indeed, there were things wrapped in plastic Baggies: faded black-and-white photos, old tax returns, faded concert tickets, and one photo (a complete surprise), the wife, the commercial photographer, her huge Polish breasts immortalized, pressed flat upon a glass tabletop but seen from underneath where a camera shuttered. Thrilled, I beheld the wife, her nipples distorted and blown out of proportion (a male bonding moment, for sure). I quickly dug deeper and deeper into the trunk, my groin pulsing like the pulsing loins of the young women I imagined in my class, thighs squeezing for me.

"It's all about character," M.B. kept saying, the waitress not far, his voice still loud, now impressive.

At the trunk's bottom, I found an old leather book, the pages well thumbed and scrawled with huge Xs, red pen and ink blots over failed stories, half-baked poetry, fragments of plays, all meticulously dated, the entries going back to the 1960s. But I dug deeper, hoping to find more nudes, not literature, pussy shots of the happy wife, Telephotos perhaps. Only I discovered a prison diary, and there a dirty little secret: M.B.'s parents were Communists during the McCarthy era. Instead of milk, they rammed politics down his throat, wheeling him in a stroller to union marches on Cooper Square, strapping placards to his back, parading him before the United Nations. M.B. was their spotlight, longing to hide itself, flying from shadow to shadow—but in vain. The diary was strident, shrill, and much like his published work. There were no Xs here, no dates. He vented fully: self-loathing and loathing for his parents, with whom he apparently failed to bond. So at sixteen (at Berkeley) M.B. sided with administration in student takeovers.

But then (I read) he was arrested for parking tickets. He got six months in jail. *The son of a bitch*. My brother, the fearsome political voice in the land of the free. He mesmerized faculty at parties (including me) with his SDS stories. But now I knew that instead of admitting his mistake, the fiction writer created a story (a bonding opportunity) to earn some admiration from his parents, who never knew about his real politics. They only knew what he told them. He was at Berkeley, and a soldier in the struggle. A paradox, no doubt, a character, surely, but this was his story, the Best of 1994.

I have no patience for creating character. If I had, I would do what M.B. has implored me to do. I'd betray my commitment to literary allusion and in the process, as M.B. says, I'd have a crack at getting my name in the back of that fat yellow book.

But another paradox suddenly unfolds, which is unfortunate. Like allusion, once you start down this road, it just builds and builds, until you have paradoxes and no story.

M.B. gets the waitress's phone number. I don't. Then she asks him, in a voice too loud, "Are you guys writers—both of you? I'm a writer too."

A wonderful paradox, no doubt, and one that will surely fill M.B.'s pen, but not mine. I'm the master of literary allusion—or have you figured it out already? M.B. (my buddy, my pal) stands for? Male Bond.

Now, talk among yourselves. *Discuss.*

Miss Mandi and Me

I want to bump the uglies with Miss Mandi, but she steps off because I'm not officially an adult. The attendance record on her desk says I'm seventeen years old. But there's another problem, one I haven't gotten down on yet. I'm only eleven. Miss Mandi is thirty-five. She's been in the army, she's six foot two, she has hair under her armpits and a voice that's boom-box bass. I know what to do with Mandi's mitten if she ever gives me a chance.

Meantime, we're supposed to be studyin' Bakhtin's Dialogical Principle. I can't say shit about questions of inter-textuality. (I dropped out of the fifth grade.) I just sink myself into this little-ass seat with the desktop up to my too-big kneecaps, checking out the people around me. There's fifteen suckers in this class, which starts every morning with ten minutes of freewriting in blue books, people all jiggling their pens. But the only thing I want to jiggle are them big Mandi tits, and Sue Ann Brown, who sits across the aisle from me. I'd like to bone her good and dry.

But between the two, today, I prefer my Sue. Though forty or forty-two (she won't tell me her real age), she's got that old lady look, that taste for young meat, boys with tight butts, 'cause she's all dried up herself. Strangely, neither she nor anybody seems pissed that I'm here, which is word-up with me.

Our multicultural reader is full of ugly pictures of people from around the world, people with dots on their heads, people with spaghetti dripping from their mouths, and African people catching fish with their hands, their half-naked butts smiling in front of some straw huts. I don't know any wild Africans, but this book is big enough for me to hide behind, to write notes to my homeboys back in Comstock. But every day I gotta wait till reader response time or else ole Mandi be walking up and down the aisle, sticking real close to Sue Ann, who sits behind me now; she's either complaining that I've shown her my yamoo (more than once) or she's kicking me in the shins.

Sue Ann, I learned after chasing her around the cafeteria, has been taking some hell-fire self-defense classes at the Women's Correctional Center. This explains the grunts I hear just before the sharp pain waters my eyes. She's just lucky that I got religion in prison. I know what it feels like to be a made woman.

Yeah, every now and then I cop that a fuck-up was made, that I'm in a place I don't belong. Maybe Mandi knows the shit, but for some reason (I can't figure out yet) she's going along with the game. When I was first given my orders to appear in this class, I wanted to step off and complain. The stupidest warden should have seen the problem, but I've begun to think that this is some *dis*, that I'm bein' set up again. (In juvenile prison they didn't call me Time Bomb for nothing.)

Now it doesn't seem to fucking matter. Doing this seems as whacked out as doing my old thing back in the hood, which was being a gangtsa rapper. That gig got me more rec-time in the prison yard, the warden's rehab, to practice my music.

You don't just become a gangsta rapper without being a murderous motherfucker, singing about cop killing, stabbing bitches, and going to the burbs to blow off some whitey's head. That's raw, that's street, and that's how I'm gonna get me some G. All them gangstas like Snoop Dogg and Ice-T and Biggie and Public Enemy, all them fuckers been running from the law, like me.

Give me a Glock and I'll blow off your A&P hole. Give me Miss Mandi and I'll make her moan for the bone; she'll scream for the cream. That's why they put my ass in here—though I think someone fucked up big time. Still nothing's gonna rock my world, y'all. I can always squeeze butter from a lump-o'-shit. Being fucked up at eleven teaches you a lot.

Lately, in fact, that Miss Mandi been askin' me to help her get some crazy boyfriend off her ass, some kind of night stalker. She shows me where the sucker bruised her up. She offers to put in a word with the warden. But I thumbs her down. My rap sheet can't stand any more heat. I send her over to Sue Ann. I got a future to think about.

Every morning, the attendance is called: Getumup, Hebblewaite, Lubjca, Mappledurah, Nintang, Nunokawa, Tinkilop, Wakhasis. It's like the cell check by the sergeant of the guard. But here in prison, it's like I'm always out of step. It's taking me a long time to realize what all these other niggers have known from the *git*: What we do in here don't mean shit. But I keep askin' myself, Why?

But one day this shit comes down which makes me ask myself something else. One night we were woke up and ordered to collect all the bugs in sight, from the toilets to the showers, ground up. The guard who woke us was sweatin' and apologizing. He didn't like us gangstas, spiders tattooed to our eyelids, doing our stare thing. Later on, a captain rolled by. When he saw us knee deep in our bugs, totally fucked up, he just shook his head, cursing out loud. Then I got the shit down cold—orders are orders!

That Sue Ann's somethin' else. The other day, she kicked my shins 'cause I sent Mandi to her about that night stalker. My shins are still all purple and shit. But I don't kick her back. Miss Mandi's been looking at me and I don't want to do anything that will send me back to the Com again. Funny, but Sue Ann reminds me of my old bitch, the one I had in my other life, while Mandi keeps acting like a little kid. She's constantly checking me out, trying hard to keep that sexy look out of her eye. But I heard the other students have noticed and it's all over the ding-dong. It's out that I'm her little pet.

Sometimes I wonder what evil brung me here. Sometimes I figure it's all my old bitch's fault, the one I slapped up, knocked her tits left and right, real gangstalike. (What's her fucking name?) I'm just pulling your chain. I'll never forget that bitch, UKRETIA. I know her evil name as well as I know my prison number: 082554687. She called herself Mermaid and belonged to the Deuce Hoover Crips, a gangsta bitch who stood up in court and said, "I'm glad your dumb ass is put away twenty-four/seven. Nobody stinky fingas my little sister."

To which I replied. "Fuck you, eight to eighty, blind, cripple, or crazy, if they can't walk, drag 'em, cause Willy Pang will fuck anything." Bitches ain't nothing but hos and tricks anyway—hear what I'm saying?

I shift in my seat just remembering that last day in court. And Sue Ann just keeps watching me, giving me that dead eye. She's started asking questions about the difference between the size of my desk and my own size. She's been wondering if maybe I ain't lying about my age. I'm just bigger than most, that's all.

I'm not totally pissed off about going through school again. Things are done different now. These big people ain't like the little ones I met my first time through. In my old elementary school, them big-ass teachers couldn't do shit to get us to pick up a pen. And if they fucked with our heads, one of us would tell the teacher to pull down the shades, saying the sun hurt our eyes. But when the shades went down, someone would turn off the lights and bust that teacher in the mouth.

But these people here, they just do whatever the fuck Mandi says, just 'cause she's calling herself professor and everyone keeps saying, *But this is college, this is college.* I'm seriously getting tired of this shit. This shit is a prison. This ain't real school. And soon I'm gonna pull them shades down, freak out, and do the nasty to some pee hole, like that Sue Ann.

I guess the first time through school I was too busy drawing blood to understand what everybody else figured out about what's right and what's wrong. I never saw what this had to do with my life. On my street, the cops were selling drugs, Mom was selling drugs, and yo, I was selling Mom's dried pussy (to buy *my* drugs).

When I dropped out of fifth grade, my gangsta career, my music, my life, stretched before me like a $20,000 lynx coat. I found plenty of clues that my dream was right: writing songs with my gang buddies, surviving drive-by shootings, writing songs about it, looting and beating people in Crown Heights, singing songs about it, burning up

Korean stores, singing about it. This all seemed to prove that I was running with the juice, like all them gangstas who now got them videos on *MTV Raps*, waving guns at the TV cameras and shit. I love that shit.

But that's all before my tragic accident with stinky UKRETIA's little sister. I misread the clues, see. It was all different from what the authorities said, calling it a crime. I just felt that it was my gangsta duty to get a little mitten if it was right in my face. I didn't ask that bitch UKRETIA to bring me baby-sitting for her six-year-old sister. If I'm in a room and them purple dinosaurs—fuck Barney—panties are on the floor, if them panties come off, *hey*: pussy is pussy. I'm only eleven years old, so I figure what the hell, stick it in, you hear what I'm saying?

It's that bitch's fault, leaving me alone so she could go out and buy some blow, crack up my nose and *yo*, a crack in my hand and the next thing I know, I end up here at Father Fleichman State Prison under the hot eyes of Miss Mandi with a stalker on her ass.

One good thing, my diet's changed now that I'm here. I no longer drink processed juice and eat peanut butter sandwiches in the regular mess, everyone banging metal trays and spoons, some guys hiding metal scraps in their body cavities so they could sharpen them up into shivs, and do their man shit. Now I go to frat parties. (Prison college is minimum security.) I smoke and drink until I puke. I swear allegiance to my frat brothers, who get into hazing, which is as nasty as that gangsta shit I did in the hood, like getting them frat bitches so drunk the entire football team lifts up them skirts to look under the hood to see how the shit really works.

But when prison school is out, I don't play. I just sit around my cell thinking that it's only a matter of time before I feel my real age. This is just something that once you learn you can never get rid of. They try juveniles as adults, but I live in fear of Miss Mandi, that one day she'll keep me after school, and when we're alone, she'll create a "bad position," which is what the judge called what I did. To keep back this hot-eyed Mandi, I've tried to be a good student.

This is another reason some of my frat boys have been dissin' me lately. But I can't deny that I'm lap-tented by the bitch. I can't deny that around the butt, Mandi is one tempting piece-o'-mitten, if I can only pull down them *dinos*, hear what I'm saying?

Now and then, there are half-ass threats to my bigness, to my sometimes position as the class giant. But most of the inmates got manners about me. They see that I'm some kind of mutant. But they don't say it. Once in a while someone tries to fuck with my head, cracking jokes, trying to make me into a cartoon, some Teenage Ninja Turtle.

But I chill out 'cause these egghead motherfuckers don't know what they're dealing with. They don't know shit about bringing a Glock to school; they ain't never grabbed no little bitch's clit, hear what I'm saying? And if she hadn't opened her mouth, and let the brown out, I wouldn't of had to smack her ass nearly off the planet. They don't call me Time Bomb for nothin'.

So I chill, but this white guy, Arty Strump (his old man made big bucks in the ink business), has been asking me if I want to fight. He's got a thing about Sue Ann, some male thing about me showing her my ding-a-ling (which sounds like a line from my next gangsta song: "Sue Ann got a thing for my ding-a-ling"). Anyway, on this day, a group of his followers gathered to see what they thought was gonna be my suicide if I didn't back off. And I would have looked to my cavities if it weren't for Mandi's eyewitness, so I stepped off, and everyone, including Arty, seemed grateful that no one had to deal with child abuse. Like, I warned them that I was only eleven. I told them, "You don't know nothing about me."

Then I went to my cell and cried. I missed my mom, which ain't real gangstalike. But I know what men can do to me. Then Mandi showed up on surprise. She spoke to Arty about my situation. She said how she was trying to get ahold of my mom. If she could get some birth certificate, something, since the warden said all he got on me was some computer paper. It might be some glitch thing, she said.

Suddenly she didn't look so hot eyed. She was using a tissue to rub my wet cheeks.

I told her to forget about it. Find my mom? Man, that lady be a 100 percent Yo Momma joke:

—Yo momma so crazy, she checks into a roach motel.

—Yo momma house so dirty roaches ride around on dune buggies!

—Yo momma head so big it shows up on radar.

—Man, yo momma shit's so big her butt exploded!

Find my moms? I got to laugh. My mom's been gone so long even them big-time drug dealers, who want to wipe her ass into oblivion, can't find her. And those suckers got connections.

Mandi just sighs and says it's worth a try anyway. Then she brings my too-big head to her heavy mother breasts and I lay on them like they be some kind of pillows, and I start closing my eyes like I done when my mom wasn't such a Yo, Fucking Joke.

I see between Mandi's bra, under her straps, some purple scratches, like nails been up there. I'd seen that plenty, way before eleven. And I feel maybe I can do something for this Mandi and her mad-ass boyfriend which she talks on and on about while rocking me in her arms. Maybe she's not that bad. Maybe she should adopt me, you know, if only she'd shave her armpits, which are a little stinky.

Now Arty and me are friends. He told me secretly that he can get me all the ink I ever need at a low price, and I plan to need it, 'cause when I'm the King of Gangsta Rap I'm not having me just one $20,000 lynx coat; I'm gonna get me a closet full and ink them every color of the rainbow—except that dinosaur shit, that purple shit, which I got a new rap about. It goes like this:

I hate you, you hate me
Let's team up and kill Barney
With a shot in the head
and knock him to the ground.
Now there's no more dinosaur.

The underground circulating library just brung me a copy of *Pasticcio*. Only it's not a food thing; it's a gift (by way of my man Strump) from Cherry Raven, a sickly girl who until this day didn't say shit to me. I smile at Raven and give her a sweet tooth over the shoulder. My little blackbird hides her head under the desk. I've seen these books before being passed around the class, during closed-book exams, and what I don't get is, Mandi takes them away whenever she finds them.

But as I flip through this book, I get what Strump promised. The answers are underlined in yellow ink, and I don't get exactly what the words mean, but I see them: *Pastiche involves the reproduction of both the form and content of a work. It involves a degree of (rather naughty) skill on the imitator, implying a certain fault, maybe plagiarism, though it may carry amusement and even instruction.*

So I don't get it. Why take our books away if this is what it is? If Mandi wants us to know *Pasticcio*, then our copying (is what Strump says it is) should be what we're learning to do. I don't get it. What do all these big people think about when they come across whole chunks of smudged yellow? Do they really "decipher" the language, as Mandi keeps asking? And what the fuck does that mean?

Gangsta rap uses everybody's shit (which is what I tell Strump). My boys 2 Live Crew got taken to the Supreme Court by some white boy 'cause they used his song "Pretty Woman" in the rap, only they was making fun of his stupid shit, and that's why the court said they can copy whatever the fuck they want.

I don't need no *ciphering* to understand that shit. I'm a gangsta, and lots of us are dissin' that pretty-woman bullshit, using our raw street talent, showing what gangsta bitches are all about. I'm eleven years old, but I know shit, which is (maybe) why the warden sent my ass to college. Maybe he checked out my mentals? Maybe my brain is too big. I'm a big kid, right?

Shit!

Now Sue Ann saw Raven passing me the answers during this test. Now Sue Ann pulls out like seven books herself and she thrusts them toward me, but just as I reach out (thinking that maybe she's making up) the bitch pulls them back and gives me a shitty grin. I go back to my test and look at the list of things we're supposed to know:

1. Epistole Obscurorum Virorum
2. Die Literarische Parodie
3. La Parodies du Nouveau

So who are all these people around me (Sue Ann, Arty, Raven, Mandi) who put themselves through a world of pain to understand all this shit? I wonder, and I know Sue Ann probably knows. It's obvious that she's been studying this as a guide to what to expect when she is freed (she tells me) from her Prison House of Language, where she says women got to put up with the *he/she*, the grammatical oppression, that is, the language of oppression, which is why she says she won't lay off my shins when I gangsta bitch. Still, I'm angry at her for keeping them answers from my hands. THANKS FOR NOTHING.

I finally got the courage to write a letter to the warden, asking for a smaller school. At lunchtime, I can hardly move. My knees are all red 'cause all day I got to keep them under the edge of the desk too small for me. Miss Mandi promises to speak to the school custodian about it (but he's not around much). She is worried, she says, about the excellence of my exam scores. Have I been getting help? For a wild minute I almost open my mouth and let the brown out, but something deep inside warns me to shut up. Here I suddenly feel safe. I have a place here and I don't want to go back and trust myself to those crazy prison people.

Strump says he has an explanation for my newfound security: "Here, Mandi makes everything an easy-to-follow process. If you wish to arrive at six, you get there by way of three by three. You see this in the way she hands back the exams, pass or fail. Here it's simply right or wrong. Nothing in between."

Still, I got to say, I wonder, Who points out that plans get fucked up, errors are made, tragic accidents happen, signals are misread (as my lawyer said): If it looks like mitten to someone like me, just a kid, it looks like my gangsta duty to do the stinky, and still, I end up in jail! Like yo, who decides?

Finally, a note comes from the warden: "You are proceeding wonderfully." Then a note comes from Strump: "Good work, not ratting on us, about the test. I put a word in at the office."

Then disaster strikes. Tomorrow I got to see a head doctor for an observation. Sue Ann caught me and Mandi in the coat closet, during a fire drill when everyone's supposed to be outside. I told her we had to talk. Mandi's a fire marshal. But for a moment I thought Sue Ann was gonna choke both our asses off the planet. She ran out of the room, weeping, and straight for the warden. She wasn't sure, she said, who was the pastiche and who was the parody: Mandi or me.

She was babbling. It didn't make sense, and I was sorry we were the cause of her disillusionment (as Mandi testified). She, my Mandi, was not trying to do any stinky with me in the closet, even though I had my winkle out (as Sue Ann knows I like to). It was all about that crazy night stalker, the boyfriend, and Mandi just figured (with her eyes all black and blue) an eleven-year-old with prison experience might be of some help. Maybe I could fix it (as she testified), but my winkle was too high a price. She didn't moan for my bone after all, and yet she was still charged with contributing to the delinquency of a minor.

But yo, I tried to tell the authorities (as my lawyer said) that I was only a minor in the very literal sense. Blame me. Check out my mentals, *again*.

Glasses

When I get up in the morning, I just lay in bed, like an old log, listening to my mom's sweet voice, singing in the kitchen like she swallowed a whole pack of angels—wings, trumpets, and all. And I like her face, all glowing, like she has a halo, all fuzzy and warm. Just like my bedroom curtains. They're all fuzzy, too, and they got a warm light shining through, showing off a pretty design, like a million ladybugs. Lord knows, everything in my room seems to have this soft glow. My walls are all yellowy and my ceiling is a mess of different colors, all for me, my private rainbow.

Outside my window, I thank God the courtyard is the prettiest in the whole world, even if the TV is always saying that the South Bronx is some kind of mess. I mean, I heard it's spozed to be so bad, they sent for the President of the United States to look for his-big-self. But he saw it wasn't as bad as they said. 'Cause he ain't never been back here. Or heard from. And that's word with me.

I got the prettiest garden right under my window. It has hedges and bushes and green grass and the whole thing sparkles in the sun, like someone sprinkled diamonds all over it. And then there is old

Mr. Hedges. He sits all day long in a big-butt chair and you can see that he must be the richest man in the world because all kinds of gold dust spills out from under his behind, gathering at his feet. Like he's on a king's throne!

And Hedges has one of those halo faces, like Mom, all fuzzy and soft. It's like God blessed everything and everybody with a special glow.

"Melissa, child. Granny will be here soon. You dressed yet?"

That's Mom. She just looks in on me and I'm real glad she lets me dress myself. 'Cause I'm pretty special, too—if I say so myself. I got a glow; you can see it, right deep in my eyes. And when I put on my prettiest pink ribbon, my pink dress, I think I belong in a fairy book. Like everybody on my street is always squeezing my cheeks and telling me how cute I am—especially Granny.

Soon as she sees me, she gives me a big hug. "So how's my baby doing?"

Then she turns to my mom before I can answer. "You been taking good care of my child while I'm gone?"

And usually Mom just whines, Everything's okay. But today Mom sounds uptight.

"Why don't you stop acting like I don't know what I'm doing?" she says.

And Granny says, "I would if you weren't such a baby your-sad-self. You ain't even eighteen. What is this world coming to?"

It's true. Mr. Hedges says that Mom is *spozed* to be too young for mothering. But it's never bothered me the way it does Granny, who is always mumbling about it.

Still, Mom sticks up for her-proud-self: "I ain't no baby, you know."

Granny fumbles with my ribbon and grumbles some more.

"Well, if you're so smart, then why doesn't this child have her glasses yet? She'll go blind for sure . . . the longer you wait."

"No I won't," I say.

"Now hold on," says Mom. "Don't start in on that now."

"Well I wouldn't have to start in on it if you'd done what you were supposed to do."

"Well, if I didn't have to work," says Mom, "I would've gotten her glasses a long time ago. It's not my fault you're too busy to help me out."

"Help you out! I've been offering to take this child for weeks—months. But every time I come over, you come up with some sorry excuse to put it off."

"Me? I wanted to go myself. I'm her mother. But I have to work. Anyway, how'd we get into this argument?"

"How? You're always trying to argue with me. That's how."

"Me?" says Mom. "You started it. What's the beef anyway? You're here! The child is here! We're getting the glasses today! End of story."

"End of story, my foot," says Granny as she flops into an easy chair, takes out a handkerchief, and wipes some sweat pooling under her chin. "That school is gonna send a social worker in here if Melissa doesn't get her glasses. And you know what that means? So don't get uppity. Without me, you'd be sorry. Oh boy, you'd be in big trouble."

"Right Mom, right Mom." My mom pulls my ribbon into a tight bow. "Now I'll be late for work. Then we'll see who's gonna pay for the glasses."

Then Mom brushes her hands up and down my dress, like she's dusting off a piece of furniture.

"Damn teachers and social workers," she mumbles to herself. "Now I gotta work weekends. I thought public school was free. Every time I turn around it's something else. Gym shorts, then a box of crayons, and pencils and erasers—where does it end?" my mom says, pushing me and Granny out the door.

"But I don't want glasses," I say as Granny scoops me in her arms and carries me down the stairs. I don't want everybody grumbling on a-count-a-me. "I don't want glasses."

"You mean, you don't want glasses?" says a nice white man, who quickly straps my head into some kind of helmet, which is like being in a bowling ball, my eyes peeking out of the finger holes.

"But you're such a pretty young lady," says the white man as he begins putting like sunglasses on me, with all kinds of knobs and dials on it. "You must have glasses."

"Now sit still," he tells me as he draws up his chair, his face smack up to mine. I've never been so close to a white man before, and even though I've heard warnings about them, all their evil doings, I was surprised. He wasn't bad at all. He had a pink glow on his face, all soft, and he even had a little halo like Mom—and his hands were all red and puffy like those angels on them church windows, stuffed in little white diapers, flying through the clouds.

He's pretty nice, I figure. He gently pokes his finger under my eyelid and he shines a light into my face. Then the next thing I know, I'm staring down a long tube, right eye first, left eye closed, and he's saying, "Now this won't hurt a bit. . . . Relax. Just tell me what you see."

"I see a bug," I say, and the white man laughs. He fidgets with some dials on my helmet. "Now what do you see?"

"It looks like, a *c-r, p*?"

"It's an *O*," says the white man. Then he turns more knobs. "Now what do you see?"

"Owww," I scream and pull my eye from the tube, making a sucking noise like a plug yanked from the bathtub. "That hurt."

I've never seen anything that big before, that clear. I swear it hurt. Even if it was *just* a letter, a *P* (I think), it sure wasn't soft and fuzzy like I was used to. I swear that *P* looked ugly, like it was skinned alive, and it hurt my eye.

That's when the white man snaps on a light and next thing I know I'm back in the waiting room—in Granny's arms—while the white man is explaining how my glasses will be ready in a few days. Then he gives me a pat on the head and a lollipop. And he tells Granny I was an "A-plus" patient.

Over the next few days, that's the joke up and down my building. That white man must've been crazy. Everybody howled with delight. Melissa, an A-plus patient. I was considered the most nervous child on the block, the one who was always turning up under people's feet, tripping over things and bouncing off the walls, and constantly knocking things over.

"Crazy white man." I agree with Mr. Hedges, who is sitting by the garden, whittling a piece of wood with his pocket knife.

A few days later, I'm shook out of bed by some yelling under my window. "Package for Three-B." It's the postman. And a few neighbors (especially Mr. Hedges) get real interested.

"Humm, it must be the glasses. Melissa!" they start screaming. "Get down here!"

"My glasses," I say, holding my hand out to the mailman while Mr. Hedges stands by my side. Everybody else is in their windows staring down at the courtyard.

"My, my," people whisper, "about time. Thought the mom let the child go blind for sure."

But the mailman doesn't hand over the package.

"It's COD," he says. "I need twenty-five ninety-nine."

"What's that?" I ask. But then Mom comes rushing down, digging in her purse. "How much?" But when she hears the price, she starts screaming, "That damn doctor is cheating us."

The mailman shrugs. "Don't look at me, lady. I collect the bucks or it's return to sender."

"Return!" shouts Mr. Hedges. "What kinda mailman are you? It's a child's glasses."

"I don't care if it's the pope's potty," says the mailman. "No cash, no delivery."

"How much you need," Mr. Hedges finally says as Mom digs in her purse, pulling up a few dollars and some pennies.

"I got fifteen," says Mom.

"Well," says Mr. Hedges, digging in his socks, "don't seem like eleven bucks is gonna make me rich. Take it."

He holds out the money, but Mom's proud-self refuses.

"Now come on," says Mr. Hedges. "Your daughter is nearly my child as much as yours. Ain't that right, sweetheart?"

I nod.

Mr. Hedges argues some more.

"Come on now. Take the money. We can't let the child go blind. We got enough trouble around here without seeing our young ones suffering. It's only eleven bucks. And if it makes you feel better, you can pay me back."

Mom finally gives in, and the mailman says he's sorry as he hands me the package. Then I turn around and promise everybody that I'll take good care of my glasses. I promise I won't play with them, and I'll clean them and hide them in a safe place at night. I get a lot of kisses for that, and people cheer and applaud from their windows. Then I run up to my room to try on my glasses in private.

I stare at them on the top of my bedspread. They got a sweet little red frame with little cats perched on the ends that wrap around my ears. I bought them red to match my pretty pink ribbon and my dress. But then something scary happens.

I put on them glasses. But it's a trick. This ain't my room. My curtains which had them pretty little ladybugs look all gray and torn, and instead of ladybugs all I see are dead flies and mosquitoes, squashed and dry. And my walls, which *spozed* to be all yellowy and like a rainbow, are all green and moldy and full of cracks and long strips of Scotch tape which keep all kinds of peeling paint and plaster from falling down on my head. In fact, my whole room suddenly looks like some old, dried-up toe scab!

I suddenly feel like puking and I catch myself in the mirror. I look sick and ratty. My pretty ribbon is nothing but a piece of old dishrag and my pink dress is half faded. I don't even look like a princess. Then I stick my head out of my bedroom window to make sure I'm in the right place.

I see Mr. Hedges smiling up at me. But he ain't sitting on no throne with gold dust at his feet. He's sitting on this old chair whose guts leak out like the stuff that leaks from dead animals. It's yellow sawdust, not gold. And there ain't no garden shining with diamonds. It ain't nothing but weeds and rocks and tin cans and broken glass and dog crap.

That's when Mom looks in to see what's up. Everybody is waiting to see my glasses. But I see that she looks ugly too. Like she's dead and no one told her yet. Still, I try to force a smile and tell Mom I love her and my new glasses. But in fact—as soon as she leaves the room—I feel sick again. Deep in my stomach.

I've never seen so many ugly things in my life. This can't be my room, my building, my neighbors . . . my everything. So I decided then and there: Until I figure this out, I'll never put on them glasses again.

You People

Smoke trailed from doorjambs and rooftops, blotting out the sun: The brightest thing on the street was a paramedic in white overalls with a red cross on his back like a bull's-eye. He wrapped a bandage around the head of an old Black woman weeping on the curb as a stretcher was slid into the back of a police van.

Rumors spread through the hood. "They cracked that boy's head wide open. Them white cops." The cops said the victim took out a knife and lunged at the policewoman. "LAPD cops, all of 'em, in bed with that Mark Fuhrman."

Three days of looting and violence passed quickly.

Mr. and Mrs. Lucce held hands and slowly dragged a squeaky shopping cart over the bloodstained street. Now Mr. Lucce's greatest fear was that one of them would slip, break a hip, and end up in the hospital for the holidays. But when Mrs. Lucce saw Mr. Jenkins and his son outside their grocery store, she smiled at her husband as she always did. The Jenkinses were sunk low in their lawn chairs, shotguns balanced on their kneecaps.

"Now what you folks doin' out in this mess?" said Mr. Jenkins.

"Ya want, I could run up some bread," said Jenkins Junior, offering Mr. Lucce a chair.

"No thanks," said Mr. Lucce. "Better you hold down the fort."

"Helluva night," said Mr. Jenkins, shaking his head as if it all were his terrible burden. "But people in Los Angeles sick of these doings."

"But people gotta eat, don't they?" said Mrs. Lucce. "And all the stores burned and closed out."

"Yes, we gotta eat," added the husband.

He swore he could still smell the proscuitto and provolone in the rotten floorboards of Jenkins's store. Only now the floor was tiled. He had been warned by Mrs. Lucce: "Don't mention it." These people overcame their circumstances. They might take it the wrong way. It's just that Mr. Lucce had lived on the boulevard so long, he remembered when Jenkins's Deli was Fiori's Bakery. And why shouldn't he remember? Even with his eyesight failing, he could still see the faded signs along this, his boyhood street: Dante's Cafe, Laccio's Drugs, Alonzo's Paper Company—all the Italians that once lived in South Central.

"Yup, that's the truth. People gotta eat," said Jenkins Junior, pulling Mr. Lucce's shopping cart into the store just as a fire engine clanged around the corner.

"But I don't get it," Mr. Jenkins said. "The burning and looting. They even hit on the brothers last night. Now me and my boy are standing guard. They're haters out there."

"They hate *our* skin, you mean," said Mr. Lucce.

Mr. Jenkins seemed busy sweeping glass away from his broken windows.

"So, why don't you let my boy run up something?" said Mr. Jenkins. "Really, you people shouldn't be out on a day like this."

"You know my husband," said Mrs. Lucce, winking. "It's something to do with floorboards and provolone."

"You mean he's still smelling my place?" said Mr. Jenkins. "But them folks are long gone. Mr. Lucce, please, please . . . don't go sniffing around here like you did the other day. Gives people the wrong idea."

"And people gotta eat," said Mrs. Lucce, her voice bubbly.

Just then, Mr. Hurley came into the store, his thumbs covered with soot. Mrs. Lucce was laughing as she helped Jenkins Junior fill a sack with flour.

"Good mornin', y'all."

"Good mornin' yourself," said Mr. Jenkins. "When is all this nonsense gonna end? It's ruinin' business."

"And good morning to you," said Mr. Lucce. "I guess it's good we live in the same building, don't you think, Mr. Hurley? They're burning out the others."

"I suppose," said Mr. Hurley. "But I didn't expect to see you people. But yeah, long as I'm super—"

"But some people are burning out their own," said Mr. Jenkins.

"Well, not me anyway. Not yet," said Mr. Hurley. "Boiler's gonna need some fixin', though. Could be cold tonight."

"That's what you said last time," said Jenkins Junior. "These poor folks came in here lookin' for canned food."

"Yeah," said Mr. Lucce. He was standing next to the son, who was hacking away at a frozen chicken. "Lots of old people in the building nearly went solid in the cold. Why don't you just get a new boiler?"

Mrs. Lucce gave her husband a sideways look. He should've known better, pressuring people like Mr. Hurley whose difficulties probably began on some plantation—ages ago.

"How about a new boiler?" asked Mr. Jenkins.

Mr. Hurley picked up his grocery bag. "A new boiler?"

Smoke filled the little store as the front door slammed shut. Mr. Hurley didn't wave good-bye.

"Such a nice man," said Mrs. Lucce.

"Will that be all?" asked Jenkins Junior, dragging the shopping cart to the cash register.

"Maybe you folks better stock up. With this mess, you never know," said Mr. Jenkins, adding up the items. "Put it on the bill, as usual?"

"You're too kind," said Mrs. Lucce, opening her purse. "But we've imposed on you people for too long." She handed over the last few dollars of the week.

"Besides," said Mr. Lucce, "it's the first of the month. The check should be in the mail."

"Hell, if you need anything, just let us know," said Junior.

On the way home, Mrs. Lucce chattered, "The Jenkins are nice people." Mr. Lucce nodded mechanically. He held open the graffiti-splattered door for the mailman, Mr. Dupee. But before Mrs. Lucce could drag the cart into the lobby, Mr. Dupee gave her a helping hand.

"First of the month," said Mr. Lucce, anxiously.

Mr. Dupee dug in his bag. "Actually," he said, "with all the craziness, there's been a delay."

"It's that bad?" asked Mrs. Lucce.

Mr. Dupee locked the boxes and looked at the old couple. "It's getting worse," he said. "It's going to snow."

"Snow! In Los Angeles?" said Mr. Lucce. Everyone seemed shocked as a lone snowflake blew against the lobby door, which was scorched charcoal black. "Maybe I'll take the dogs to the park."

"We don't have a dog," said Mrs. Lucce.

It howled all night. Snowdrifts banked over the hoods of cars; clouds of steam rose from the hot ash smoldering under the ice-covered streets. Mrs. Lucce stuffed newspaper and towels into the cracks of her windowsills; an icicle hung from the ceiling pipes. Mr. Lucce fell asleep in an armchair, his feet propped on a pillow in front of the kitchen stove.

This was totally nuts. Snow in California. Mrs. Lucce kept dialing the Weather Channel. But the line was always busy.

Then the snow stopped and the sun was well above the smoky rooftops, the mercury pinned to its bulb. Mrs. Lucce woke, fell asleep, shivered, and woke again. She was on the floor under a woolen blanket. Mr. Lucce's head was thrown back, his mouth wide open, eyes closed.

"Danny? Danny?"

The oven had gone out during the night and Mr. Lucce's blanket had slipped off. Mrs. Lucce rubbed her husband's face until the pink came back.

"Damn boiler again!" he said.

"No lights, and no gas," Mrs. Lucce added. "Maybe the whole city is down."

"No, it's them, I tell you. The gangstas."

"What are you trying to say?"

"Oh, right. I forgot. *Their* circumstances, of course."

"It's because of our skin . . . you're saying?"

Mr. Lucce opened the refrigerator. The light was out. The milk was bad and the eggs had burst. "People gotta eat." His false teeth clacked. "My denture glue? I can't even boil water."

"Danny, stop thinking about your stomach. You can't shut me out. It's because of our skin, you think."

"No, everyone and everybody, they're just wonderful. And delightful. Delightful and wonderful."

"Don't be stupid, you. I'll show you."

She picked up the telephone: "Mr. Jenkins. Thank God. Our boiler, our oven, everything's out. Could you have your son bring some hot coffee, and fresh bread?"

There was static at the other end.

"Mr. Jenkins?"

"I'm sorry. It's crazy-busy down here."

There was more static.

"Excuse me? Hello? Are you there?"

"Sorry—"

"Hello? Hello? Anyone there?"

"Hello, Mrs. Lucce. I'm sorry. Dad's busy, but if you can wait, I'll run up as soon as I can."

"Oh, you will? How wonderful."

"What now?" asked Mr. Lucce.

"They're busy, but Junior will come up as soon as he can."

"Busy?"

Mr. Lucce looked out the window and saw a policeman turn the corner by Jenkins's store. His footprints were the first and only ones in the freshly fallen snow. "Busy, huh. Funny how snow sticks."

"What's the snow got to do with it?"

"If they're so damn busy, why aren't there more footprints outside the store? Look out the window."

"No, I won't. I won't look. I'm sick of your suspicions. You've ruined my life."

"My suspicions. Maria, what do you think the looting and burning are all about—*you*?"

"That has nothing to do with it."

"Right, I never heard you people this and that in Jenkins' store today. I imagined it, like a lot of things."

“Oh you’re just trying to get even because Jenkins won’t let you sniff around the place.”

“Right, that’s another thing. Whose side are you on, anyway?” said Mr. Lucce. “You just want them to think I’m a good-for-nothing.”

“Now you don’t trust me, either.”

“No, it’s them.”

“Know what I think? We’re going to end up in an early grave if we don’t do something.”

“What?”

Mrs. Lucce went to the window. There was still hardly a footprint in the hardening snow.

“I better go down myself,” she said, “even if I slip and break a hip.” Her husband agreed to watch her from the window.

Mrs. Lucce dragged her shopping cart down the long hallway. Funny, she thought, the lights were on. Still she hurried, afraid the Jenkinses might close for the day, so she left her cart at the top of the stairs; it was too heavy to carry down in a rush.

“Am I glad to see you.”

Surprised, Mr. Dupee looked up the stairwell at the cart. Then he turned back to the mailboxes filled with green checks, checks that he stuffed into his mailbag.

"You're surprised?" said the mailman. "But I thought you people would be under the covers, staying warm."

"We will, but first we need a little money. We gotta eat, but the gas is out and the heat is off."

"That's what you people think about?"

"That's a funny way to put it, isn't it?" said Mrs. Lucce.

"You sure crack me up."

Mr. Dupee locked the boxes and was knee deep in snow when Mrs. Lucce realized: The check! "You forgot the check!"

"There's a delay," he said, without turning around.

Mrs. Lucce climbed back up the steps. Then she got a whiff of cooking fat and she heard bacon crackling in a frying pan, and a steam pipe hissed behind a neighbor's door.

"Danny?" She found her husband hacking away at some frozen milk, sucking on the ice chips.

"Where's the shopping cart," he blurted, "the food?"

"The cart? Jesus, I left it by the steps, but when I came back, it was gone."

"Gone? You mean stolen?"

"I don't get it. I heard someone cooking, I swear, and the hall lights are on and I think there's steam in this building and checks for everyone but us."

"What am I, an idiot?" Mr. Lucce grabbed the phone. "This time I'm catching them." He put down the phone.

"It's dead," he said. "They cut the line. What are they doing to us?"

Mr. Lucce looked under the kitchen sink.

"What are you doing?" said Mrs. Lucce.

"No, what are *you* doing?" said Mr. Lucce, pulling out a toolbox.

He grabbed a crowbar and got on a ladder. Then he banged on the pipes, knocking the icicles from the ceiling.

"The bastards." He hit the pipes again. "People have to eat," he cried. "Don't they know?" He swung his crowbar with all his strength. Then his ladder slipped. He fell and his false teeth were knocked loose and into a corner of the room, with a hard slap, like a hockey puck.

Mrs. Lucce walked over, picked them up, wiped them clean on her coat, and tenderly fixed them back into her husband's mouth.

To Break a Nigga's Neck

Being they was putting me down anyway, being they'd tell my moms the same shit they told her when they killed my brother, that the sucker escaped with the bed and everything (handcuffed to it 'n' shit), that some guard went cronz crazy—just had to defend himself—and that the body was blasted so strong it just hung itself up in the tree on a hill two miles from the projects where the escape was made, being it wasn't just my brother who vanished quick from the world going through a door left too easily open, but so many others who just flew off the street corners and killed themselves in some alley, being they was planning to put me down anyway, no quicker they chained me to the bed with my burned skin than I decided to break loose from here. But now . . .

He tells me Z captured a boy too.

"What kind?" I ask.

"A Guy . . . from Guyana." He laughs at his own joke. He's talking to Z on the other phone.

"Does the boy speak English?"

"Better than you," he says.

"And how old is he?"

"Older than you."

"Is he bigger?"

"Yes, he's much bigger than you."

"So, what's he doing?"

"Z says he has a gold tooth and he's polishing it. But Z wants to know about you."

"Tell him I'm flying a kite. Tell him I can do anything."

"Well, Z says his boy is tossing hair balls into a can. Z says you don't stand a fucking chance."

The blindfold was off, but like it was hard to see much in the dark, hard to see with a bloody eye, but I could tell that I could slip the chains off my wrists, squeeze myself forward enough to get them round my waist enough to drag the bed, inch by inch, to slide the bed that had rollers to freedom. If in the morning they showed it to the reporters as evidence, it would be amazing even to my homeboys, who never thought that I had this kind of juice, that I couldn't escape under such impossible circumstances (as the report would put it).

"So, what's in your note?"

"You'll see. You have to sign it."

"Will you tell her where I am?"

"We can't do that."

"So, how's the boy?"

"Almost lost him. Z is real sloppy, the way he goes about it. He wears a mask. He uses a strong chemical—sometimes a plunger."

They'd call it street justice, a gangsta thing, niggers just shoot themselves in the back, no matter what they do. There was no way I was waiting for them to come back, thudding down the loose steps in their jack boots, to bring me back, to blow my throat into bits, not even staining the floor because they got these chains to hold me still, and this mattress to soak me up, the way they done my brother.

It was too much, this waiting every day for the same time, each day like a year, waiting for them to come down to the basement where I was blindfolded, to jump me like pit bulls, with pit-bull teeth and hungry jaws, like I was already a bag of pus, gnawing at my guts and chewing on my bones, not listening to my screams, day in and day out, 24/7.

But I don't regret nothing. I held with my posse. I didn't give them one name, not one name. I admitted, I sold crack, I tore down anybody that tried to get in on my trade, I sold guns to rivals, if the price was right, I stole police cars and went for rides, and I didn't pay any fucking insurance, I didn't pay the pig tolls and I got the others to shut them down too, because they took too much, laid off too many niggers who couldn't make the tolls themselves. And so I admitted, I went to Internal Affairs to bring me in, before it was too late, knowing I'd squealed too much and too long on too many payoffs, but I'm a gangsta with heart—no one puts shit in my mouth—no matter what they did, they couldn't get me to turn in the Deuce Hoover Crips. They didn't get shit, so they stuck me in this hole to finish me off.

"So, how does the boy feel about Z?"

"He's too sloppy. The other day, the boy rushed him with a breakfast fork. Stabbed him twice in the belly."

"But aren't you talking to him on the phone?"

"Wasn't nothing. He's been stabbed before. But now, Z says, the boy looks like he got five police clubs stuck up his asshole."

Officially, the report said my brother got himself killed in the hall, that after he choked the guard with his chains, he tried to get himself into the elevator, but seeing how the bed on his back didn't fit he decided to run for some stairs, but that was such a lame story to anybody with half a brain, still, it didn't make a *dif*, being it was in the report and the newspapers said that's what my brother done; he used his spit and blood to oil the rusty wheels on the bed to sneak up on that guard, forcing him to turn over his machine pistol and to call an unmarked car to zip him back to South Central, which he wasn't able to do being it became so necessary for another guard to blow him away in a hail of bullets, so he couldn't make it back to terrorize the decent folks no more.

"Mine's sick," he says.

"What's the matter?"

"He won't eat."

"So what," says Z. "Just speak to him. Tell him we can steal a new boy, a child. We could grab him and keep him, rub him with gas, burn him and make him moan."

"You know," he says. "You're a dumb-ass."

Standing in the morgue at my brother's feet, I knew it wasn't what the report said, I bet he didn't figure they'd execute him after all the beatings he got (so bad we closed the coffin), but that's what went down: They shot him stone cold and made up an escape which my brother was in no shape to make, so I swore to my moms if these fuckers ever put the touch on me, being I was now the man of the house, I wasn't being killed just standing around; I was gonna surprise them by ending the story just like they wrote it.

That's why as soon as I got myself into that hall, my arms aching, and I saw that guard sleeping just like they said when my brother split, it was real easy to wrap my chains around that bastard's neck that was sucking for air, his eyes bugging out, not believing that such a cripple like me, chained to a bed with a broken body, could crush his windpipe so easy, like he was unable to believe that what was now happening was what happened a year ago, according to the official report, only now this shit was happening for real, this time he was being killed, *for real*, his tongue hanging out even though he pretended like he was dead, dropping his arms to his side, hoping my scorched arms would show mercy and let go.

So, like, it was the pigs' own report that was mapping out my escape, the ones who investigated the crime scene, measuring elevators and beds and guard posts with the sole purpose of putting together the pieces of my brother's death, with diagrams like math lessons making my escape a snap, a replay of all that my brother supposedly done.

And what if I was blasted away? What if the halls rolled more tape than rugs? What if this was going to be shown on some TV news as an excuse for all the shootings—past, present, and future? Rodney King had tape. And that L.A. dick Mark Fuhrman had tape, said "niggers beaten and killed for years," said they beat the niggers so bad they clawed and streaked the walls with blood. So fuck it.

> *"At breakfast, Z says, there was another attack from the boy. The boy said Z was a shit who watched too much TV. He said Z fed on innocent kids, blah, blah. So I told Z, I said, that's the problem with capturing one of these boys. You must yank out their hair, wrap their balls in wire . . . and pack their wounds with sea salt."*

I punched the elevator button. If the bullets burned me, fuck it, the assholes just wasted their lead because at least I made them sweat, drip, and run. I made them see what a true gangsta is all about. Fuck it. If they were taping me, if this was all part of their game, fuck it. I quit playing because in the hands of death the gangsta's gotta show what being a man is all about. Fuck 'em—let them wear out their hearts trying to catch me.

Before the elevator opened, I crouched with my bed on my back like my ancestors crouching before the slavers, like my beaten ancestors dragging the plows on their backs to the master's whip, crouching in the dust, waiting, and when the elevator doors opened, I leaped inside with my ancestors' fury coughing through me, and even though I was badly beaten, like a beast, I crushed that guard's face, left him soaking in the rug while I planned my next step, knowing no one gets away no matter how slick he thinks he is.

But like, we got a saying in the hood: You know what time it is! That's the time it was, time to change their bullshit plan, like I knew a ride in the unmarked car, like my brother supposedly done, was a ride to kingdom come, so I had to come up with my own trick and fast, because when those elevators doors opened again I'd be looking on the main hall where I needed to situate myself behind the guard with his back to me, just like the report said, pulling up my chains without letting out a clink, to stick them into his back, making like it was a gun, then blindfolding him with my own bandages and making him get into that car, into the backseat, cursing and kicking while I told the driver that I was getting into the back myself and if he turned around or stopped I'd blast his brains to soup.

I saw that the sucker did like he was told, drove off thinking I was still in the back, when I stayed behind with my bed, taking a back way instead, no more a part of the policeman's report. Chained to my bed with its wheels, I was on top, using my mutilated arms like oars to roll myself down freedom's way, like a monster chained to a block, I went down; I was ready to smash them if they waited at the alley's end. I went down like a nightmare, not caring if they rolled tape infrared.

It was then I heard the machine gun blasting at that unmarked car, how they opened the back door so the one I'd bandaged fell out in front of them as they took a closer look, blasting away, smiling, thinking they got one more nigger trying to walk off with their bed, sure that now as they turned this one over they realized (at that moment) they killed one of their own and I got away, realizing that now they'd have to call my moms, tell her that her youngest boy had been locked away like the others, but "lamentably" the keepers of law and order let him get away and now that he was out, instead of asking her to identify the body, to cry her eyes out; instead of that, they'd have to swallow hard and stare at this Black woman while I flew into the night, my chains flowing from my body, running from the barking dogs and the searchlights, the oppressors' fury sweeping the rooftops of L.A., driven by the words they would now have to use to inform my moms, the words not in their script, the words that would have to be forced out, one by one, like pulling teeth, the words I could predict because I am the fire by which my brothers can warm their hearts and load their weapons to plan the liberation. I am alive and I listen to the words fired at my moms—proving that no one can play me—the words that I forced out of their mouths, the words they'll never put in their reports, the words by which I let my moms know that we shall overcome, we shall get to the promised land despite the words that took them so long to say:

"Ma'am, just tell us where the boy is. You see, he's run off and it's our duty to serve, protect, and break a nigga's neck."

Zap-a-Ho

He was shouting into the phone, "A bum, there's a bum on your fire escape." Jumping from my bed at 2 A.M., I looked out the window. "What bum?" I figured Julio sent one of his boyz to scare the shit out of me.

"There ain't no bum out here!" I said.

He started laughing so hard he dropped the phone a million times. I believe he laughed so hard he dropped to the phone-booth floor. Then I knew this nigga needed a urine test.

"What the fuck you on?" I said.

"Not a bum," he wheezed into the phone. "A bom-ba. A BOMB!"

At that point I felt a strong flash on my face, a bright light, and a hot blast that knocked me into my room ass backwards and over my bench press. My 100-pound barbell hit the floor.

Julio was still laughing on the phone, the smoke rising from a milk carton that was now in flames on my fire escape. Neighbors looked out their windows. There was so much smoke, my mom came in asking if I was okay, until she saw me on the phone giggling with

Julio. Then I got my ass tossed around the house. That woman did laundry work at 5 A.M. in a hospital.

But that's Julio, making things up, amazing me and everybody else. Even as I speak, he may or may not be dead. How can I know for sure if I'd never seen his ass in a funeral box, or went to a cemetery and stared at his grave? Six years after the bombing, I was on my way to help my man Chilly P. scratch a new rap song. I bumped into Julio's first wife, Anne. She told me that one night Julio was doing his usual drugs, drinking and driving. He ran a stop sign with his new wife and three kids in the car, ran slap into a sixteen-wheeler that killed them all. But how could I know (for sure) that this wasn't just another Julio trick? Just like all those postcards I got from places like San Juan, Puerto Rico, Australia, and one from Venice, New York—all postmarked on the same day.

I knew Julio got his army buddies around the world to mail these cards to confuse me and everybody else. If he was so dead (and flat, as Anne said), who sent me the Julio New Year's card from Hawaii? What the fuck! Once we were friends, weren't we?

When we were kids, we cut school after my mom went to work and hung out in my room. We made egg salad sandwiches and watched cartoons. He tried on my clothes and never returned the ones he borrowed. He said we were brothers, and that's how we got to be called the Leather Boyz. We bought the same jackets, pants, belts, and caps. We even made the same money selling the same drugs to the same people outside our school, at the same price. Everybody got the point about us, except those who couldn't help notice that we weren't exactly EXACT: Julio was Rican and I wasn't. So they said I'd better give up that "brother" crap. They also said we weren't just boyz; we were dick suckers.

But with Julio, that was a big mistake. He didn't represent. He always bragged that he'd suck a dick as fast as he'd suck a pussy. In fact, he bragged, if he ever had a son that was a faggot, damn, he said, "He better give me a piece of ass, too!"

That was Julio. Outrageous wild, so out there everybody had to stand back and laugh. He told them all, gangstas and wannabes, in broad daylight. He held out his hand on the school steps and dared anyone to put his meat right there, right in his hand, right then. His insanity was his shield. He took out his dick in the street and in the playground. He pulled on it and screamed, "Mees-ter, I'm coming!" No one did nothing to stop him.

Soon after that, that summer, Julio gave Little Bruce a big idea. Bruce said his girlfriend Patty gave him blow jobs in the park by the Deegan Expressway. Patty was twelve, fat and pimpled. She had buck teeth. But for Julio, a dick sucking was a dick sucking. He said the thought of those little teeth scraping his glans sent shivers up and down his horny spine. For a few bags of pot, Bruce let Julio hide in the bushes to watch Patty do her tongue thang.

I didn't know anything about Patty until I got to Marco's Pizza. The boyz were busy hooting and huddled around a bunch of Polaroids. There was Bruce getting his penis yanked by Patty. Her eyes were yellow from the camera flash. Julio had snapped them in the act. The pictures were spread between empty Coke cups and Bruce sat with a sausage, half bit, making sucking sounds in his little mouth. Froggy was the loudest at the table, talking about how she'd better swallow it when it was his turn. Everyone was flipping coins. Someone was next and suddenly Julio was saying it was me.

It was his idea and I was Julio's man, his homeboy. I got a snapshot and I was told to go to Bruce's roof. All I had to say was, "Suck it, Patty, or I'm giving this picture to your pop." Patty was waiting for me. Everybody knew her old man already beat her for no reason at all, beat her bad with metal and held her wrists to the oven and shit. As long as she was around, guys with snapshots caught her on the way to school in the morning for a quick valve cleaning; they got her outside school at lunch, on the way home, and never let her spit it out. Right quick they expected her to drop to her knees between parked cars. And she did, for a while, until it got out of hand and guys all over the hood were begging (and paying) Julio for a Polaroid. Then Patty disappeared and we all figured she just chose her pop's licking over licking ours.

That was Julio's joke and now he was the man with the ideas. Suddenly he knew how to deal with the bitches. If he could get everybody's dick sucked, guys figured, what was next? Julio talked and they listened. "You want to get a bitch hot in the twat?" said Julio. He showed us his pinkie nail, grown out and curved like a claw. "Use this to flick that clit," he said. I saw Froggy's mouth drool with possibility.

One night, Julio dressed up in a garter belt and black stockings. He taped his penis back so that only his pubic hair showed between his legs like a girl's mitten. He danced like a stripper in Tuffy's garage. Stoned, the boyz hooted as Julio shook his naked, hairy ass square in their faces and they reached out for him while he pulled back and played the bitch master.

Now Julio was wearing a gold ring on every finger. Each time he popped a virgin, he said, he added another. He bragged that he even popped the eight-year-olds, the blind and the crippled ones, too. We believed him; we believed everything. He brought girls to Tuffy's garage for us, runaways he'd found God knows where, prostitutes. Then he'd somehow fill them with sleeping pills, and let everybody line up and do their business on the floor until the girls bled. (Some guys brought sharpened pencils.)

Condoms? Some had them on. But Julio? He told us to spit on our dicks, stick it in and don't worry, just like him. "Fuck AIDS," he said. Before long lots of guys were dipping into the same holes, dipping in with Julio, who was always first served, first come. He brought the bitches, right? Once in a while the pills wore off, the girls woke up and tried to fight, but then Julio administered the cure, a few whacks until the bitch was back on all fours, as he said. And those that screamed about the cops, they were the ones most in trouble with the law themselves, and Julio knew it. He knew they weren't doing shit about anything. Lots of them were on probation and didn't want to go back to jail, away from the kids they probably got in places like Tuffy's. Often they themselves were torturers, arrested for beating and robbing their mothers and fathers, grandmothers and grandfathers. All of us were scum.

"Scum fucking scum," said Julio.

One girl, Sugar, had scars all over her body and she pierced anything that jiggled—her nipples, her underarms, the crease in her eyelids. She was hard core and she fucked us straight up, no pills and no cocktails. She laughed in our faces. She brought her girlfriends and soon we were outnumbered. Then one day, Little Bruce went to

Tuffy's and was tied up by Sugar's new gang. What they did to his dick with burning creams and cigarettes, we swore it was our secret until we died.

"The bitches," said Froggy. "They took over Tuffy's."

The bitches sharpened their Afro-combs and hid them in their hair. They hid razor blades in their cheeks, and made guys freak for their foreskins. Sugar even got a gun and locked us out for good. Julio offered to clean everybody's pipes himself until he came up with a plan. But no one wanted to hear shit. Maybe Julio was gay or bi-or tri-; that was okay, said Froggy, "as long as everybody got to bone some dry pussy." But now Froggy warned Julio that the real brothers were going to cut off his Puerto Rican dick and throw it from a roof if we weren't back in Tuffy's, rapido.

I was also getting suspicious looks from everybody. I'd just spent a few days working with my mom at the laundry and somebody found out. But I needed the money to make a demo tape. I wanted to sing songs about the shit that I lived. But I knew that these niggas would never think that I could be a hard-core rapper and tune up my craft, not if I was putting some dick in my mouth, especially Julio's.

I knew this shit was like crack to them. They'd go nuts and beat my homo ass. But as far as I knew, yo, rap music and hip-hop were always about boyz, about pussy getting and pussy cracking. It's always been about boy shit, boyz talking to boyz about what they'd do with (or to) other boyz. Like the D. Geto Crew, their new song:

> I'll spread your ass on a fuckin' hanger
> and slam your shit with a hot poker
> a fuckin' club. . . . I'll bang you with a
> fuckin' dick, a fuckin' 12 incher.

I loved that boy shit, that rap. But I knew that with Julio this wasn't just going to be something in a song. These niggas were serious. If Julio didn't get everybody back into Tuffy's, he was dead in a heartbeat. And so I stood by my man's side. He asked and I promised. I swore I'd help him with his plan.

"The Amazing Zap-a-Ho?" said Froggy.

"That's Julio's idea," I said.

"Zap-a-Ho's getting us back to the pussy shack?"

"That's it," I said.

We all waited for Julio in a store room under Marco's Pizza. We sat on cases of peeled tomatoes, flour bags, and blocks of mozzarella cheese. I screwed in a red lightbulb myself. Julio wanted a big show, and even though it was a little dark, everybody felt Julio would come through in the end. He was Mr. Surprise. And now everyone was restless and wanted me to explain this Zap-a-Ho. How will it lay Sugar and her bitches low? Then they reminded me: If Julio didn't show up, they'd plug my ass with fire clubs. Then they'd burn me.

I told them Zap-a-Ho might be like a robot thing, a big handlike thing with like a paddle thing that worked like a laser that fixed onto a plate on a bitch's back, following her around so when she stepped out of line, whack—bang she'd be set right.

"But I ain't exactly sure," I kept saying. Everybody knew Julio couldn't build any robot thing without a factory. I believe they were getting ready to damage my nappy head when Julio's voice boomed from the cellar walls, and Julio jumped from a stack of tomato cans, hitting the floor in a perfect gymnast split. He wore purple eye makeup and red pants that sucked onto his overinflated crotch. He also wore a silver cone bra like Madonna. It was clear that the show had begun. He waved a long, beaded, silver stick around his head. Like a game-show host, his voice was bubbly:

"Yo, all you bum-rushin' tramps out there, you know, those a you bragging on the nut but not getting none?"

Julio bopped Froggy with the wand. And Froggy laughed along with everybody else. This felt like fun.

"Yeah, you know the ones I'm taking about, all a you no-count homeboys trying to get more than a butt that's boomin'!"

I was laughing now, doing my part as Julio said, flicking the lights on and off so it was like a strobe as Julio pranced and strutted and bopped everybody now, right on the head.

"So yo, if your nasty ho is making that dash, that funky go-go—and I bet the bitch is—all you gotta do is roll with my Zap-a-Ho, drop them underpants in two spincos flat. I put my life on that!"

"You will," Froggy blurted. "How's it work?"

Julio put the wand to Froggy's shoulder.

"How it works? All you do is grab that bitch up and whack her head with the Zap-a-Ho and I guarantee one hundred percent she'll be in L-U-V, she'll be bringing you forties and a blunt. But hey, if you don't believe me, ax my cousin Pedro up there in the Projects. Cuzz, how you doing there, keeping your ladies fixed?"

Julio disappeared momentarily behind some flour bags, and when he came out, he had his bra off and a baseball cap on sideways. He was doing a night at the Apollo, a quick change. Even his voice changed as he became Cuzzin Pedro, sounding like a cartoon pappy:

"Well boo-ya, once I got me my own twenty electrode Zap-a-Ho, man them pussies went def jam. I mean, thanks to my amazing Zap-a-Ho, I bust all them juicies and loosies, like twenty-four/seven."

Julio went off into the dark again. Froggy began to chant and everyone joined in, clapping hands: "Puss-EE! Puss-EE." Julio reappeared, swirling a long cape around his head.

"That's pussy two times," he said. "I told you all—I'll put my life on this."

"So," said Froggy, "when we gonna see the fucking thing? The Zap-a-Ho?"

"Got it right here," said Julio, pulling the cape off the floor to reveal what looked like a head brace with frayed copper wires dangling from the neck cuff, all hooked up to an old plug.

"You just wrap this monster around a bitch's neck," said Julio. He showed us a heavy lock. "Then you snap this sucker shut and you can bet that no bitch is getting away with shit, or she'll get herself an electric shock that will make her pussy twitch."

"You just plug it in?" said Froggy. "Like that?"

"Like that," said Julio. "Zap, and that woman is on her back, legs spread, pussy ready."

Froggy handled the device, asking me to make sure that the plug wasn't connected.

"Now all we gotta do is test the sucker," said Julio. "That runaway bitch, Sugar, with all them scars, I bet she likes pain. And if it works on her nasty ass, it'll work on anyone's. Slam-bam, and we're back to

Tuffy's with them meat eaters between our legs, like the good old days. What do you say?"

That got Froggy thinking. "We don't want to kill the ho, do we?" He fingered the frayed wires. "Are you bullshitting?"

Then somebody else said, "But what if I want to take my bitch to a party? This shit is too big and you need a plug."

"Hey," said Julio. "Chill out. You're also talking to the maker of Blam-a-Ho and Snag-a-Ho. I got plans for Port-o-Ho, brother, a little thing that slips on your woman's wrist. I'm thinking about remote control, a twat box! You can zap a bitch from across the room."

"You're saying we got to kidnap Sugar and test the sucker?" said Froggy.

Just then I had to say something before things got too serious. Julio was my friend and all, and because I loved the sucker, for sure, I didn't want to see him go too far. He was crazy enough to try this thing. He (and I) just meant to fool these suckers, but Julio was really getting into it.

"Look, boys," I said, "listen, you can't plug in Sugar. An electric shock can slap a three-hundred-pound man to a ceiling like a bug."

Froggy caught on fast and he grabbed the dumb thing from Julio's hand and plugged it in to see what would happen. Luckily, he dropped it in time. The wires sputtered and burst into flames.

"You've been playing with us," said Froggy. The brothers were at his back now.

Julio gave me a hard look that I'll always remember, like his eyeballs were thumbs on my neck. Then he took out a remote control (which looked like the one from my mom's TV). He smiled and bowed. Then the red bulb popped and there was a sharp flash and a bang and tomato sauce and flour shooting up all over the room. Dense smoke followed and we all ran out of Marco's heaving and dry coughing.

That was the last time anybody ever saw Julio. The crew hunted him for months. Finally someone got the word. A local army recruiter boasted that everything he'd heard about Julio only convinced him that this boy was going to have a solid career defending America, using his natural gifts to blow shit up.

"Fact is," said the army recruiter, "that boy Julio is already in the desert in the war." He imagined that each time Saddam Hussein lost a tank there was a little Julio behind it, not just gunpowder. Julio must've paid him to say that.

The recruiter then handed us forms and told us if we joined ourselves, we might catch up with Julio on the inside. Any takers? But nobody wanted to get Julio that bad, not even Sugar, who packed an automatic pistol and swore that she was carrying Julio's baby. And I myself, well, I just hope he is really dead like I heard because the thing is:

After my man Julio popped off the earth I wrote this rap song (I said I had a plan) called "Zap-a-Ho." It's been in all the newspapers and on TV. It's been attacked by all kinds of organizations, like the National Association of Black Churches and Women Against Pornography. They're calling me and my record trash. Still, my album went platinum, so I can't say I want to see Julio's face right now and like, split the profits! No way!

Fact is, my profits are already being drained because suddenly lots of those girls from Tuffy's are claiming on the *Jenny Jones* show that I tortured and raped them myself with that Zap-a-Ho, which was Julio's idea in the first place.

Besides, I recently got a call from my mom. Something about the dead come back to life. She was still at her Wash&Press shop (which I paid for), and she said I should look in the tumbler of her newest, her biggest, her just-shipped washer. She said she wasn't stepping back into that store. She wasn't saying anything. She wasn't blaming me if it was true. I didn't know what the hell she meant, but I figured if she sounded so freaked, a tough lady like this, a big woman who hauled thirty-pound laundry sacks all her life, I'd check it out, carrying some protection. I grabbed a kitchen knife and went to the store.

"Mom," I said, "leave up the metal gate."

This way anyone from the street could look in, just in case. I never liked seeing all that gang graffiti sprayed on my mom's windows, but it's better not to piss anyone off by rubbing it out.

It was in the corner, still in its packing crate, half opened, taking up a whole wall, and its door was flipped out, where my mom said she froze, before backing out. Her desk telephone was off the hook. I took out my knife and approached the machine, slowly, and ever so slowly, grabbing a lamp, I shone a light inside the stainless steel tumbler that sparkled newly finished and polished, and I saw it: A milk carton with black masking tape was deep inside and hard to reach, like something stuck up on the roof of a mouth; and I knew immediately, slowly using the tip of my knife to close the door, to get to the phone, to call the bomb squad.

But as soon as the phone was back on its receiver it was ringing, as if whoever was calling planned it this way. I picked it up and it was Mom again, back home, looking at her mail, she said, and staring at this postcard from Saudi Arabia with red smears like lipstick that read something like *BUM. BUM.*

A policeman in a bomb suit reached in and crumpled the milk carton in his fist, after probes and scans showed that it was empty, just a prank. But the fact that this came in the crate, which was factory sealed in China, was a clue to something, he said—and they'd look into it. I didn't mention the postcard.

Not long after that, in fact, my mom closed the gates on her washing machine business anyway and she went back to working the night shifts in the hospital laundry. I soon followed, folding other people's clothes, busted from all kinds of legal bills and broken lease fees on Mom's store, not to mention the money I still owed those private detectives I'd hired to find Julio's grave, some kind of marker.

The Tooth Fairy

He sees me/he sees me not.

It really doesn't matter. I first */sawn/* (past tense, see) him in *Central Park*, a little magazine, the best of the Small Press. It was a *short* story, a little thing; and if I hadn't /sawn/ it, it would've turned into paste in a recycling bin, along with its precious acknowledgements page, boasting (with a heavy hand) local, state, and federal funding: SEE YOUR TAX DOLLARS AT WORK.

It was called "Teeth," and even my secretary was in the acknowledgments. I felt betrayed by her, too, and I made a note to make her life miserable. I'd submit thick, handwritten faculty reports. The pencil, smudged like eyeliner, would make her eyes tear, drip, and muddy those evaluations until they pooled on her desk and slipped into her lap, like a lump-o'-Gak!

And this semester I'd rub the little bastard raw with his little story in his little magazine. I'm a lifer at this great City University of Health, Education, and Welfare. I have tenure, while he's a nothing, a part-timer that can be toppled. I'll observe his teaching, and do a Siskel and Ebert, a thumbs-down. I'll *fix it* so he never passes me in this hall again. My salary is twice his for half the work, and under the Freedom of Information Act, you can see this on the Computer Highway.

YOUR TAX DOLLARS AT WORK: Both of us, eyeballing each other in the hall of this great university, each beneficiaries of this great public dole, each an affiliate of this great English Department where even a secretary shares the acknowledgments page with you (taxpayers all).

And what shall I say to the little bastard?

"I've /sawn/ your little piece, your 'Teeth,' in *Central Park*?"

It was my idea and he stole it. It was on this exact spot. We often chatted here, making distinctions between us and them, our colleagues whom we pitied because they (unlike us) were resigned to publishing meditations on the comma splice in such places as the *Journal of Basic Writing*. While we, the department's creative writers, were busily responding to the contemporary modes of thought, feeling, and speech. We knew that we were the ones fated to slip the Prison House of Language. We knew our work would be greeted with disdain, at first, until we'd proven that we were not destructive to the National Literature, but *re-creative*.

This is exactly how we felt on this spot: It is a necessary condition for the continuance of literature that the language should be in constant change. If it is changing, it is alive; and if it doesn't change, then new writers have no escape from imitating the classics without hope of producing anything good.

I stole that from T. S. Eliot. It was actually the impulse behind my "Teeth," my idea, which I shared with this little bastard. I told him that I was planning a novel about teeth, the first of its kind. It would be on the leading edge of the Trash Phenomena. It would be on the cutting edge, but it wouldn't fall off the cliff. It would be intelligible, and readable, reflecting my bouts of gum disease, which bloodied my pillow, my history of pus and abscess, impacted wisdoms, and my green teeth from too much experimental penicillin in the Bronx in the 1950s. Like David Salle, I'd be high brow and low; I'd include the Greco and the Roman, the great teeth epochs of the Ancient World, and the great teeth of all time: First President George Washington's wooden teeth.

These are under glass in Mount Vernon, the family mansion where slaves (their teeth, too) are buried out back where once potties dappled the landscape of this now publicly funded National Monument. There's even a text under glass, a national literature of sorts, detailing Washington's dental history in language as wooden as the teeth, lacking words like */sawn/*, which I would use to bring my teeth alive, to begin a new literature of sorts, one that would inspire novels on hair, nails, toes, the corn, the cramp, the kibe, the bunion, the vagina, and the winkle.

I had no idea that the little bastard would be so literal. His "Teeth" (a story and not a novel) focused on a man who woke to find that where once he had flesh as fine as breast milk now he's covered with clacking teeth that frighten his family like Kafka's bug and threaten to pierce those who would console him, like a woman he beds who endures the very teeth that, inward turning, threaten to breach his walls, his abdomen, which keeps his guts from spilling onto the floor.

But despite my colleague's attempt to be new, his story doesn't even use */sawn/* or its ilk, and he regurgitates Kafka. God knows, women don't need more stories about risking their guts for l'amore—the tooth prince.

So the little bastard stole my idea and couldn't resist the Hurray for Hollywood—the happy end, which is brought to you by the people of Pepto-Bismol. I myself should bash in his teeth (which is an obnoxious addition to my novel).

But I see him/he sees me not.

Not *he*, but *me*, stole the Teeth. I'm the thief. And I don't feel bad about taking his Teeth. I smiled when I passed him in the hall and he smiled back. He has tenure, after all, a job for life, while I'm hungry. All I need is that one ground-breaking story, that O. Henry Award. Then I will have a better life than him. Anyway, I've read *his* work, and I know he would never tell a story (like me) about a stolen story from the victim's point of view who (it turns out) is actually the perpetrator (me). I live and die by the words of Senator Lloyd Bentsen. "Sir, I knew T. S. Eliot. He was a friend of mine, and believe me, you're no T. S. Eliot." Well, neither am I, but . . .

I knew Donald Barthelme when he was a teacher at this great university (where, once a student, I now teach too). It was here that he did create a national literature while dipping (like me) into the public dole. YOUR TAX DOLLARS AT WORK:

I wrote a story (a dream) of raping a little girl in a stream, and sitting with Donald in the bay window of his brownstone, for all to see, two writers at work, he read my story and said; "Where's the little girl?"

"It's a dream," I said. "She's not a character."

"But she's been greatly wounded," he said. "She'll have much to say."

And at that exact moment, I thought, I wouldn't have thought of that. And since I ruined my Teeth in *Central Park*, the end betrayed my mentor (whose own endings include an ETC., a herd of porcupines, and a piano slaying its player) this time I decided my story would be unlike anything ever brought into the Open. I would blaze the footsteps of yet another genius and role model, a fellow artist in New York's SoHo, who in days of old spray-canned walls and declared I AM THE BEST ARTIST. Everywhere he went, people knew: he printed his declaration on his shirt, pants, cap, and tie. I AM THE BEST ARTIST. And soon, he was in every tabloid; and if you go to SoHo now, you will find him the proud owner of a boutique sporting its own line of denim: I AM THE BEST ARTIST jackets and jeans.

I WILL BE THE BEST WRITER.
I WILL, I WILL, I WILL.

I subscribe to T. S. Eliot's maxim: "Immature poets imitate, mature poets steal." I also know that T. S. Eliot's maxim is, in fact, its own best illustration, stolen as it was from Emerson's essay "Shakespeare." Therein, Emerson says of Chaucer (whom he calls a huge "borrower") that "it has come to be practically a sort of rule in literature that a man, having once shown himself capable of original writing, is entitled thenceforth to steal from the writings of others at his discretion."

I am no T. S. Eliot, sir, but I knew Donald Barthelme. There are no less than six credits on my college transcript attributable to my work with Master Don on my master's degree. These (and other documents heretofore mentioned) are available under the Freedom of Information Act for your perusal.

Q. Haven't I heard this before?

A. Yes, you have.

Q. But what about this? Have you /sawn/ this?

This is the eagerly awaited novel by a writer who, since 1960, has been responsible for stories so distinctive and original as to redefine the form.

Q. Does this sound like something fated to bless your book? your own novel?

A. It does. It certainly does.

Q. Well, those words actually graced the book jacket of your master's work *Snow White*.

A. I know it well. Master Don brilliantly intermingles naturalistic voices with those of the fairy world. It was *form defining*.

Q. Great. Let's call the following Exhibit A. And please, as you gaze upon the clip below, note well Master Don's masterful use of subheads that violate traditional narrative conventions. Roll the tape!

Reaction to Snow White's hair: Two older men standing there observed Snow White's hair, black as ebony, tumbling from the window. "Seems like some hair comin' outa that winda there," one said.

Lack of reaction to the hair: "You know, Clipschorn was right I think when he spoke of the blanketing effect of ordinary language, referring, as I recall, to that part that sort of, you know, 'fills in' between the other parts. . . . That part, the 'filling' you might say, of which the expression 'you might say' is a good example, is to me the most interesting part. And that's why we pay particular attention, too, to these aspects of language that may be seen as a model of the Trash Phenomena."

A. Yes, I studied with Master Don and I have a master's degree.

Q. Yes, and fruitfully so. Now take a look at Exhibit B. ★Note subhead and fairy. Roll the tape!

Further extract from my manuscript, descriptive of the Pooka, his journey and other matters: Ladies and gentlemen, this is Jim Casey, Poet of the Pick and Bard of Booterstown. Approximately half of the company at this stage joined their voices together in boisterous noises of amusement. Suddenly Casey turned 'round and presented a stern face to the company.

What was I doing? he asked.

The only answer was a loud laugh.

Well, I will tell you what I was doing, he said gravely, I will tell you what I was at. I was reciting a pome to a selection of my friends.

Poetry is a thing I am very fond of, said the Good Fairy. I always make a point of following the words of Mr. Eliot: A good pome is a tonic.

A. Yes, I studied with the Master.

Q. Yes, and fruitfully so. But did you know that on the back of Exhibit B the blurb actually reads:

> Written by Flann O'Brien, *At Swim-Two-Birds* is an underground classic published in London in 1939. . . . Like Beckett, O'Brien has the gift of art, which . . . they . . . both . . . learned from Joyce.

Q. I rest my case.

A. But who are you?

I felt a tugging at my bookbag. I looked down the empty corridor. I heard a knocking at the door of the great English department. The party responsible for the knocking was not to be /sawn/. (Neither was Mr. You Stole My Teeth.)

Q. It is "I."

A. Oh, it is you. Well . . . be pleased to join me. Welcome. It's seldom that I am honored by a caller in the middle of my workday. Where are you?

Q. I am already at your ear.

A. I heard a small voice that was sweeter by far than a clap of a waterfall and brighter than the first shaft of day.

Q. I am standing here.

A. It is a queer standing. I can't see you.

Q. I have come to visit you, and to spend an hour in fine talk and to enter in a colloquy with you.

A. It is an odd place for a colloquy. For soon my students will appear and see me engaged in folly with thin air. Still, you are welcome. But your name, sweet sir? Is it a secret?

Q. My correct name is Fairy, the Tooth Fairy. And yes it's a secret and a fine one, but one that is so big each of us may share it with the other. . . . Is that fair?

A. Oh, yes, my sweet fairy!

Q. You dissin' me, muthafuckah? Who you callin' sweet, you bastard, you reader. Raise up. I'll fuck you up twice real fast! You think anybody really be talkin' like "Be pleased to join me?" Damn, that shit's not even dope, hear what I'm saying? I stole that shit myself from Suck-My-Butt O'Brien and his lucky-ass charms! I'll take whatever the fuck I want and you don't like it? You feelin' stupid? You feelin' froggy? You wanna leap? Where I come from, either you smokin' or you git smoked! Hear what I'm saying? I'm ready for a throwdown 24/7. So fuck you and your whiny ass shit about writing new, makin' up some new lang*widge*. Suck my nut, money, you and your */sawn/*. EU, you're so big and strong. I bet you moan for the bone. You scream for the cream. You bend for a friend. I'll rent your asshole, motherfuckah. I'll make you my girlfriend. You think putting slashes around one word (/sawn/) is gonna make you a prize writer? Shit, you gotta have something really raw for them O. Henry judges, which is why I wrote this whole story. I didn't speak up till now cause I wanted you assholes to see what fresh, new, original lang*widge* looks like!

You ain't heard nothin' like me. I'm not your regular tooth fairy come into your window. If I'm in the room and there's some mitten, I'm gonna get me some stinky finger. And you talkin' about lang*widge* being fresh and shit. I learned your shit till the brown came out my mouth. I went to y'all's City University, part of the Second Step Program, hear what I'm saying? They called me Time Bomb in prison. 'Cause I'm deep, money. I'm into punctuation and them stupid-ass English teachers can suck my dick. I'm one of the elite, the top 95 percent.

This whole fairy thang is some *bow*shit I made up to get PAID. Hear what I'm saying? My real thang is rap, gangsta rap, and my agent says I got something so new, so raw, so street, I'm gonna get enough G to set Mr. T bumpin'. I'm gonna be wildin', stylin', maxin', and relaxin'. 'Cause I'm the king of Gangsta. But right now, until I get my demo togetha, I'm doin' this fairy thang, hear what I'm saying?

'Cause I'm phat, muthafuckah. And I love to get that G from them stupid-ass/gap-tooth/piss-pot muthafuckahs who leave their shit right under the pillow. 'Cause I got to get PAID—hear what I'm saying?

So chill out, home. If you got this far, maybe you're a brother—and you know these people got congressional hearings on my lang-*widge*, gangsta rap and shit. But how come I don't see no hearings on y'alls /sawn/ and shit? Maybe they worried that a rapper like me, on welfare, sucking that public tit, on that public dole (just like y'all), shit, maybe I'll be creating some of that National Literature. SHIT, T.S. IN THE HOUSE, Y'ALL! My boy T.S. put it in your face: In a hundred years, that nigger says, English could be as remote as ancient Greek. Shit, I bet y'all end up talkin' like me. You got farm boys hooked toe to floor on *Yo MTV Raps*, gettin' cornholed, wearing baseball caps on backwards, wearing G in their teeth, goin' "Yo, yo, yo." Biggest buyers of rap music be those dumb-ass burbins! (Only I hear them white girls don't like being called bitches.) Don't dis yo' sis! Fuck, you don't even know the difference between a mitten, a bitch, a ho, and a trick. Bitches can suck my yamoo. I'll twist their clits, a labia on toast moe-foe. You already made up your mind about me, but if you reject me, I'll yoke your ass, I'll give you an eye jamming, I'll herb you, and don't think I don't got your address.

So don't reject me now. I got my eye on that prize, Mr. O. Henry. Don't dis me now. 'Cause you do, and I'm gonna know it's 'cause I'm Black, muthfuckah; and I'll have your ass all over the ding-dong. I'll have Reverend Sharpton at your door with a big-ass bull horn: NO JUSTICE, NO PEACE. I'll slap yo tits left and right. I'll do a Glock on your A&P hole. I'll bump the uglies.

Way I see it, your balls should be tight as leather now, your pussy hi and dry. You know (and I know), if you do run my shit, all kinds of folks (on the congressional level) will be pissed off. If they see that you be using funds—local, state, and federal—to support my lang*widge* (!) your ass be in a world-o'-pain. That's why you shouldn't be fuckin with lang*widge*. That's why I told you I got something so street, so raw, I'm gonna be part of a whole new craze.

Anything really new (as my boy T.S. says) is "greeted with disdain, at first."

That's why I know very soon I'll be making more G than any O' Flann/Don/Sam/James/Brien ever made. 'Cause my sandwich tastes sweeter when I'm sitting on a tomb. So you come to South Central, the South Bronx, South Side of Chicago, South Philly, and all them Souths where my homes be hangin', you hear what I'm saying? And you come straight up to my crew, Five Deuce Hoover Crips, come up to Coyote, Locito, Pookie, Mermaid, and say you won't run my shit and see if we don't take out your teeth with a screwdriver—twice real fast. You got heart enough for that? Answer me that!

A. As a matter of fact, I don't understand two words of what you said. I don't know what you are talking about. Do you know how many dependent clauses you used?

Q. I do not.

A. Thirty-five in all, and each of them contained enough information for a colloquy in and of itself. And there is nothing more horrible than the compression of such filth that should last for six hours into one wee hour. Tell me, did you ever study Bach?

Q. I AM THE BEST WRITER.

The Digital Hood

```
5HI = 0
10 DMA (20), B (20)
15 FOR I = 1 to 20
20 READ A (I)
25 IF A(I)> HI THEN HI = A (I)
30 NEXT I
35 PRINT   HIGHEST VALUE IS,'' HI
YO HI = 0
```

So, whassup wit' dat?

I hear what you're saying. That's the first computer program I wrote. It searched two groups of numbers and found the highest one in each group. I was eleven at the time and I didn't even have a computer. We were on welfare since my mom was busy selling her crack—*foe-one-foe*—to get some crack. You hear what I'm saying? But I didn't need a computer to know the program worked. It worked in my head, like that, because I cut school. I took trains to the city to them superstores, Barnes and Nobles. I got all the computer books I needed. Later for the public library. They always had signs: CLOSED, BUDGET CUTS.

So I learned computer language faster than the white boys learned gangsta talk, being they buy more Snoop Dogg than the brothers. In fact, I spoke BASIC before I rapped gangsta myself, all that home slice and he say/she say. Like, I speak more cyberscat than gangsta rap, which makes me no count in the hood! I'm the only sucker I know who even got a computer. And I only got it 'cause my Cuzz in South Central L.A. did a Rodney King on the Wiz, looting me a nice CYBEX ICARIAN VII. You got to have family to get ahead in the world.

I used to be into graffiti, y'all, running with a crew in the South Bronx. So I was real cozy with the idea of using other people's technology to get my name across. Like, after I raided them railroad yards and bombed them subway cars with spray paint, I got to see my tag *Scorpion* traveling overground and underground though mazes of rail and tunnel. So, yo, I had my own Internet long before I knew what the shit was. So, like . . . it was real easy for me to get dope with the idea of using some real technology to get even *knowner.*

Once I was hip that the Net got over 30 million assholes on-line, and it's growing 10 percent every month, I realized like, whassup? That's the way to let the world know I'm alive. I had a dream and all I needed was a phone, which was easy 'cause my block still got these burned-out buildings with hot AT&T boxes. So like, *yo*, I hooked up my CYBEXY VII, my laptop, and I was ready to mess with people's shit.

I left my graffiti bombers to run with a new crew, them hackers and phreaks on the VX exchange. And I'm talking about running with the Masters of Doom, Chaos, and Hellraiser, bad *moe-foes* and white boys all of them. Which is why they call themselves Cyber*punks*. But yo, in the hood, a punk is someone who rents his asshole. A punk is a raspberry, and so you never want to be called that—no way, money. And that's where I'm at, so I put it on the wideband: You better call me Cyber*gangsta*. Or I'll jump salty. And you better dig: now that I'm on-line, them happy days are over. Now that I got my phosphene boiler, I'm slamming my mimetic weapons into my core, I'm punching my console and I'm rustling your data. I'm screwing with your credit, *hear what I'm saying?* Now that I'm interfaced, I'm gonna probe and rape mankind's extended, electronic nervous system. I'm gonna make America's monochrome nonspace all mine. And don't you even smile about it.

I know you thought, like, Mr. Rogers was at the core of your own digital neighborhood? But now that I'm running with the juice (I got my crew with five separate landlines) we're gonna turn your shit into the *digital hood*. Now y'all gonna suck butt 'cause we got these simple programs, like logic bombs. And these suckers will sit in your computers, keeping an eye on your machine's internal clock. Then one day . . . *plick*. You get it straight up and nasty:

```
YOUR SYSTEM HAS BEEN CRASHED BY THE MASTERS
OF DOOM. VIRUS INSTALLED BY SCORPION. GOOD
NIGHT, CHICKENHEAD!
```

And that's only the beginning of the ugly shit that can (and *will*) happen to you in the digital hood. Once you eyeball your system's slow decay, you will dwell on it; you'll become filled with nagging self-incrimination: If only I'd been more careful with whom I interfaced. . . . If only I'd locked the gates, PEM-ed myself in. . . . If only I'd closed my windows . . . like in them real housing projects. But forget it. Certs ain't nothing but a breath mint. Nothing can stop me, and as I key this, I already feel your fear on my line, on the myoelectrics, translated through my carbon studs. You're all mine, butt-wipes. My neon projector barrels are already aimed straight at your heart. At night, under the full moon, I surf the crest of the invading programs. Then I rise through your towers of data and burn the bitch down—word to the mothers!

And all those re-up assholes on my Bronx street corner who sit in hogs all day listening to phat beats, low riding, leaning, and selling crack to make some G, those gap-mouth suckers who bump the uglies with my moms, they can all kiss my ass. I don't need a gat, a Glock, a burner, a cronz, a drive-by, and lead in my stomach to make my G. I already got more money than the Cypress Hill Gang or any of them superstar gangsta rappers who like to wave guns at the cameras on *Yo MTV Raps*, singing songs about "How It Feels to Kill a Man" or selling Sony CDs that got finger-snapping lyrics that say "Bitches ain't nothing but hos and tricks"—hear what I'm saying? I don't need that shit to make my G.

All I need is one headlong rollercoaster ride on a program that makes me a money laundry—one cyber-cleaning megabuck on-line cash transfer to my own convoluted electronic credit slot in a Zurich bank, the Cyrillic alphanumerics reeling down my monitor, the zeros multiplying until my final squirt transmission cuts behind the core command to gobble up the bank's glitch systems, the distress calls. Then I'm rich, you turkeys.

Only, when I say ICE (Intrusion Countermeasure Electronics), the assholes on my street think I'm talking about Ice-T or Ice Cube. They think I'm gonna break into gangsta song like them American Music Awards. And they already think I'm a gumby because I don't hang with the homeboys. They call me a faggot because I don't wear no head rags or vee-in, or put gangsta spiders, like tattoos, on my eyelids.

(My mom wants me off the streets, and so I sit in the rubble in the basements of the burned-out buildings, the scorched brick in the South Bronx, watching the pulsing yellow pyramids, the 3D pixels, votels, and boxels reflected in the crystalline glaze of my VR goggles, my four eyes, my glasses.)

But like, in data space, I could be a girl if I want to. There, no one calls me a faggot. The Net subtracts the human voice. When you're bodiless, nothing is at stake. I'm only a UNIX programmer, speaking C++ without an accent. The keyboard is the great equalizer. It's better than a Glock .45 caliber, because combat on the Net is like Lamdamoo. There are no bruises here and, in cyberspace, everyone can hear you scream.

So I try to tell these Bronx assholes that my 40 HEX electronic zine got more power than all the calibers they got strapped under their baggies and hoodies. Still, they say I'm lame to the bone. They say I'm a cripple, a half-stepping sissy boy, a lame brand, and they say it straight in my face:

> "Dumb sucker have no girls, don't know where anything is. . . . Stone sucker, hanging around your momma all that time. Dedicated to d' homefront. You like a schoolboy chump . . . stupid,

ignorant, hide in d' books all d' time. You square to d' wood. Don't get high, don't smoke no weed. Can't fight or nothin'."

And what can I do about it? You think I'm gonna profile? Most of them shooped my moms, so yo, money, *whassup*? I don't want to talk back and end up with a Colombian necktie, which is what the gangstas do: They cut a sucker's throat and pull the tongue through the cut. Now run and tell that!

And yet, yet, my Cuzz in South Central thinks I'm gonna be the King of Cyber*rap*. When he got my Cybex, he got two. And now we conversate on the IRC. I teach him everything I know. He's family, you hear what I'm saying? But I think living in L.A. with them movie stars fucked up his mind. He's always on my line, fucking with the 40 zine, sending me cyber songs, lyrics he thinks will make us the first cyber rappers in history. He says we'll be bigger than the Jerky Boyz. He says ain't no one ever heard nothing like us before. Cyber Scat meets Gangsta Rap. He says we'll be pure VR, our faces neon animations, shivering on high-definition television screens, the intricate patterns weaving with hypnotic frequency into America's living rooms. Just one click, he says, and we ain't *in* the music industry, we're interfaced.

But I say, *yo*, slow down home. It's good to have family cleansing my fiber optics, my subprograms scanning my machine, blocking anything that might threaten *my core*, but I don't get a thrill from this shit. He thinks I want to spend my life singing to the metallic beat of some synthesizer? But no way, I don't sing. And I know that he keeps saying if my voice sucks, we can always computer-generate a def chirp. And he keeps pushing me. He just sent me what he calls a cyber*rap* duet. He says we're partners and his opening rhymes will set the tone. He calls his rap, "Assume the Position":

> Cyberbores will kick it, this rhyme it is wicked
> Those who are POTS will get evicted
> A hacker will read you, take you & break you
> Now it's time to rhyme, can you relate to
> No one to trace you, def data for ransom
> Crash priority override, dope enough to make ya holler

And here is where my Cuzz says I'm supposed to cut in, to take over the rap in rapid-fire, double-time verse:

> Yo, yo. Let me take it from here Nigga!
> Excuse me but I think I'm about ready

to get into what I'm about to
I'm speakin' to folks who have
no fucking clue
So listen carefully 'n' I'll phreak it down
Merrily, merrily, happy happy 40 Hexed and
Over-zined, pleased with all the bits and
bytes my brothers have employed
Masters of Doom, y'all, VX parameters measured
slick and smooth, phosphene boilers, burning
chrome, throwing down the Net, totally a yes!

Assume the position: Hackers & Phreaks first!

But I can't do this shit, even if he's family. And I put it on the E-mail (Cuzz@rant.comrap). I don't want to be the King of Cyber*rap*. I just want it known: I'm the first, and the best and the baddest Cyber*gangsta* in town. And I let him know that he better not try to sell my shit to some Sony asshole. It's my creation. I'm the Master, I'm the Father of Cyber*gangsta*. And if he ever plays dirty with me, I'll slam my mimetic weapons into my core, I'll punch my console, and turn on the ICE. I'll tumble his butt into a simulation matrix, a 3-D chessboard with every keystroke a checkmate.

So listen, I don't need to croak for my lunch. I've said it once and I'll say it again: I've already clicked into my credit. I've got whirlwinds of light to spend in banks all over Zurich. I'd rather be a demonic intruder pounding on someone's electronic door. I'd rather be a cracksman probing the cold spiral arms of America's military computers. Now that's a thrill. And once you've tasted it, like I have, once you understand what I've done, my cuzz, nobody (not even you) will ever call me a gumby again. You hear what I'm saying?

Like one day, I created a virus, a Trojan horse, and I called it Mamma Jamma. Then I turned it loose on the Net and within minutes military computers nationwide felt the sting of my thing. It was a massive assault, my cuzz. Computers at MIT Artificial Intelligence, Lawrence Livermore National Laboratory, and NASA's Ames Research Center were under my gat. And once inside the U.S. Army's Ballistic Research Computers, my Mamma spread to other workstations like a real flu. And then there were hundreds of Mammas slowing down the military machines, bringing them to a halt. My virus was so nasty, it knocked on the electronic doors so fiercely, the Pentagon swore they were being invaded by a foreign power. They were so afraid I was taking Top Secret missile data and spreading it over the Net, they even disconnected their computers. They went off line for a whole month.

You hear what I'm saying? Little E-light, the me that everybody calls a no-wit skeezer, Scorpion, I beat down the entire Army of the United States of America. Just think of it, my cuzz. Think of the assholes, the gangstas that did the Rodney King and burned down South Central. The chickenheads torched their own homes, their own streets. They even burned out stores owned by the brothers. They bugged out, you hear what I'm saying, drinking the forty-ounce, and they went the nigga route. They went cronz crazy, putting lead into little kids and old ladies, brothers and sisters who went outside to watch the fireballs lick the dark sky.

But just think what would have happened if only half these niggers were wired! Just imagine what wall-to-wall niggers on the Net—nineties niggers—would have shown America about who got the power and who don't. Just think what in-ya-face gangstas on America's information superhighway can do to this country. Think about all that LAPD data just waiting to be rustled and hustled, busted and disgusted. If we want to do something about Rodney, we gotta do something about that! We could shut the suckers down, you hear what I'm saying? I mean, think about all them parole records, early-release forms, and all them computers that open and close them prison gates and doors where all our brothers, the hard-core gangstas, are just waiting to let America know: If you want to know about us, you gotta know Ice Cube's rhyme: Every cop killer ignored they just send another nigger to the morgue.

That's why I gotta let the home slice know. Cyber*gangsta* is the way of the future. Niggas gotta give up the drive-bys, the emergency rooms and funerals. No more kids caught in the hot lead, the crossfire over drugs and turf. There are endless corridors, cooperate galaxies on the computer frontier, filled with loot. So we don't gotta kill each other for some Nikes, some hogs, some G, or some eight-ball jackets no more. We can do our gangsta *thang* right in America's nonspace. And I, *Scorpion*, will lead the way. If you'll only listen to me—your Master, the Father of Cyber*gangsta*, I'll show you. If only you'll stop calling me a raspberry and lay off my mom's crack, I'll give you the power—like that.

But I know you won't listen to me. I know you. You don't even read books and you kick my ass because I do. You slap off my glasses. But you can't get on the information superhighway if you can't rustle data. If you can't read, you can't Web-crawl through Gopherspace. Do you *butt holes* hear what I'm saying? I can show you what I got, if you'll listen and learn:

```
MESSAGE NUMBER 4480 IS 11 LINES FROM CYBER-
GANGSTA (SYO) TO DARK STORM(SCO) AT 18:38:
27 ON 03-MARCH-99.
```

MUST CONSERVE SPACE. I AM CYBERGANGSTA, FAMOUS IN SOUTH B.X. AND IN THE NEW YORK PAPER FOR MY PHONE COMPUTER PHREAKING. I AM VERI IMPRSED WITH YR SYSTEM. I CAN BE OF GREAT ASSIST TO YOU. TELL ME WHAT INFO YOU NEED. CAN GET ANY PHONE TO ANYTHING. CAN RUN DMV VIA TERMINAL. CAN RUN INTERPOL VIA TERMINAL . . . CAN RUN AIRLINE TKT VIA TERMINAL . . . CAN RUN PHONE CO. VIA TERMINAL . . . HAVE MANY PRIVED ACCTS . . . CAN CRASH SYSTEMS WITHIN 20 MINUTES OF REQUEST TO DO SO . . . WORD UP, MY BROTHERS.

CYBERGANGSTA @MIT,CEX,SAT

The Rules

Up and down the tree-lined streets automatic sprinklers snapped on all at once with a sharp, metallic click, spitting water carousels over red dirt newly planted with signs: JUST SEEDED. Rows and rows of reproductions, identical Victorian homes with authentic-looking gables and turrets, made up this new development. The freshly painted gatehouse stood empty and dark. FOR SALE, everywhere Kevin Pope turned, it was FOR SALE laminated to Queen Anne windows bonded with packing tape. Even the private road was unpaved.

And why the hell were the street signs blank and the mailboxes identical, rows and rows of them, without house numbers? Kevin circled and circled, and as far as he could see, up a long hill, everything was the same: The trees, the bushes, and the flowers in clay pots were all cropped exactly alike. So much so, in fact, that Kevin's car felt as if it weren't moving at all. He imagined astronauts twirling in zero gravity.

He was lost, he knew that. But the longer he drove, the more frantically he circled, bopping his horn now and then, sooner or later they'd find him. This was a *private* community, and he knew what that meant. Here the living wasn't just easy. "Private" meant one thing to him: Nigga, that spinning red light in your rearview mirror is not a UFO.

PULL OVER
DO NOT EXIT YOUR VEHICLE
YOU'VE ARRIVED

Arrived? What did that mean? These were not real cops. They were private security guards from some bullshit company that used names like Global and International on their tin badges, and dressed themselves in black Fascist shirts and phony police caps to make these assholes who paid for privacy believe they were safe from "outsiders."

Still, Kevin knew that even bullshitters were dangerous, out to prove something, and if he took a beat down now it would be very bad for his royalties. His wallet-sized "Black Man's Survival Guide to Search and Seizure" made it very plain: There are two different realities. If you're white, there's one reality. But if you're Black, and things get tense, chances are you're the one who'll end up sucking road with a police boot in your back. So when you're stopped—when you're Black—be prepared for the worst. Then follow the rules: Number 1: Do not try to talk your way out of the situation. You can't. Number 2: Look the officers in the eye and speak respectfully so they don't think you're hiding anything.

Now this phony police car was already at Kevin's window and he was about to ask permission (Rule Number 3) to move his hands from the steering wheel to retrieve his papers from the glove compartment, when this Universe Security man smiled and said, "Actually, we were hoping you could help us."

Kevin was just waiting for the punch line. He could already smell a mind-fuck coming his way. Still, he said politely, "If possible, sir, my pleasure."

"I bet you're looking for F-Daddy, aren't you?"

Then this Universe guy sipped some coffee and sprayed it onto Kevin's windshield. Great. Kevin ignored it. These suckers didn't know who they were dealing with. He wrote the book on this shit.

"Officer, matter of fact, yes I am."

He was just about to ask for their help when they pulled away, and through the back window Kevin could see the coffee guy handing his partner what looked like a wad of money.

"Yeah, yeah," Kevin mumbled to himself. "Rule Number Four: read the guide." But then he looked up at a nearby gable, and a curtain moved in the window. At the end of the flagstone path, like at every other house, black wires hung like spaghetti from the doorbell. Then he thought he heard footsteps inside the house as well as whispering. A door slammed. The motherfucker was bailing. In his line of work, Kevin had seen it before. But with these row houses, packed tightly together, there was no way to the backyards.

"I hear you. Please, I just want to talk."

Suddenly, the front door whipped open. Blocking it was not a booty-shaking video girl, but an old lady with a teacher's bun on her head. Was this F-Daddy's woman? No way.

"Pardon me, but are you looking for someone at this address?" asked the lady.

"Come on," said Kevin. "Do you see a number on any of these crazy houses? I'm just looking for F-Daddy. So please, if he's paying you, I'll pay you a lot more."

"Well," said the lady, "if you're lost, please go back to the gatehouse and they'll direct you, I'm sure. Bye-bye."

The door was closed as fast as it was opened. All the way up the hill, lawn sprinklers snapped off, all at once, as if planned to send him a message.

He banged the lady's door. "Smallie's been killed. He's dead."

But then Kevin got a grip on himself. The rules, remember. Number 5: There are good cops and there are bad cops, but all cops have to make arrests to get promoted, so your job is to avoid giving them a reason to slap on the cuffs. Even if you're doing nothing wrong, they could always drop a disorderly conduct on you. Kevin knew better. He got his cell phone and left a message with his editor's voice mail: Need money, fast.

He then drove over the hill, where the Universe Security had disappeared. And indeed there was one structure unlike any other structure, set apart on a circling dead end, surrounded like a bull's-eye by the only patch of green grass in this construction rubble, this moonscape.

"Now keep your head low," said the security guy. Kevin was stuffed way down on the floor of the cruiser's backseat.

"You sure about this," said Kevin, "because when I knocked, I didn't hear a dog."

"It's a very quiet dog," said the security guy's sidekick. "You just make sure we get the money."

"Five hundred a pop," said the security guy, nudging his sidekick. "Isn't that so?"

"No," said Kevin, his neck beginning to ache. "Two hundred and fifty. That was the deal."

"You sure?" said the sidekick.

"Here!" Kevin tossed his cell phone into the front seat. "You call my editor. She said two-fifty."

"What magazine was that again?"

"What the fuck difference does it make to you?" said Kevin. "How the hell would you know about it? You follow gangsta rap?"

"I think he said *Fart*," said the sidekick.

"Noooo," said Kevin, "it's *phat, PHAT* Magazine. Anyway, what time does F-Daddy walk his dog? It's getting dark."

"That's why it's good you came to us," said the security guy. "It's not a race thing, but if our clients saw you crouching in the bushes, someone's ass would be on the line and it ain't mine."

"Right," said Kevin, "so how does F-Daddy do it in the dark?"

"I told you," said the sidekick to his pal. "Now you pay up."

The security guy handed over a wad of dollar bills. Kevin sat up in time to see the money exchanging hands. He'd seen this before.

"What's with you guys? This money going back and forth?"

"Hey. Keep down. He might see you."

"We're just betting, which can't offend someone like you," said the security guy.

"Like me?" said Kevin as he checked the flash on his 40 mm barrel lens.

"What you do," said the security guy. "I mean that bullshit you guys do. What do they call you now—*stalk-erazzi*?"

"You guys will shoot a corpse if it pays."

"And if I don't pay you?" said Kevin. "What will you do?"

"You'll be eating dirt," said the sidekick.

"And you ask me what I do? Shit, have you guys ever made this kind of money before, for one hour's work?"

"Actually," said the security guy, "this is more than a week's take-home for me."

"Now you hear me," said Kevin. "Like, when I get up on some bad-ass rap star with my camera, one of them that's decided to change his image, maybe you know the kind?—one of them rappers that's suddenly singing church songs, who got himself a Coke commercial and a breakfast cereal with his new wholesome self—I try to catch this kind of sucker with his woman, you know? Then I get up on him and start whispering as he walks away. He tries to ignore me, but then that's when I start my thing. I start saying things about his old lady's pussy, you know—then bang. That sucker loses his head, he loses control. Then I shoot the pictures. Sometimes I even record these suckers foul-mouthing me and—bang. I sell that stuff to the tabloids worldwide. Right there, my friends, you and I are looking at an easy fifty thousand for one night's work. And you know, of course, that rapper who lost his cool is off those cereal boxes; another role model bites the dust."

"Is that F-Daddy's story?" asked the security guy. He handed Kevin a Thermos bottle filled with rum and Coke. "Take a sip."

"Well," said Kevin, gagging on the drink. "At this point, the less you know, the longer you'll live."

"Yeah, but look at the money you can make. Maybe we can work for you sometime?" said the sidekick.

"Well," said Kevin, handing him a small camera, "if you can snap a few photos for me, I might toss you guys a crumb."

"Now I'll be damned," said the security guy. "As they say in the movies, your man has just left the building. But you're in for a big surprise, homeboy."

"I'm betting on that," said the sidekick, handing his partner another wad of bills.

"You guys crack me up," said Kevin, opening his door, a block behind F-Daddy. He watched the cruiser go over the hill.

A camera in the dark meant trouble. Kevin couldn't afford to blow the shot. He might not get another one. So now he had to get close, come face-to-face with the bastard. He owed it to Smallie's mother. He'd promised, hadn't he?

At the press conference, at her Bronx tenement, surrounded by the pancake antennas poking into the sky from the TV news vans, she choked back tears, "My boy's not a gangsta." On each arm, her weeping daughters kept her from collapsing. "He was just spinning records, making music, my boy. Why did they shoot him like that?"

She fainted, and Kevin nearly missed his opportunity to snap her, knees folding like Gumby. But then she held out her hand to him, and he took it instead of focusing. She knew that when they were kids in junior high, he and Smallie were friends. Now this thin, short woman with owl-eyed glasses invited Kevin into her apartment. He got lucky. This was an inside exclusive, and the other photographers quickly booed him. But Kevin turned on them, discreetly flashing his middle finger behind his back.

Once inside, the daughters squeezed wet Kleenexes onto the mother's swollen eyes.

"It was all a mistake," she said. "He didn't mean to dis anybody."

Still, it was too late. On Smallie's last album, *I'm a Non-Violent Man*, he had a rap song about Bishop Shue, the president of East L.A.'s most notorious crew, the Clan, real *jump me in* gang-bangers. Cops said the gang traveled with their own body bags and toe tags, saving the coroner's office time and money.

"You don't mess with an organization like that," said Kevin, "especially if you're someone like Smallie." To them Smallie was just an East Coast sissy-boy singer. His crew didn't have the right juice.

The mom agreed. Smallie's jail time was a weed bust, a few days in Riker's Island, and that was nothing. But Smallie's record company built it into more to make Smallie look like he was straight off the streets. "Fact is," she said, "my boy didn't even write his own raps. His agent, a white man with a Rolex, bought them. Look at the lyrics, the copyright."

One of the daughters handed Kevin a CD. Nearly the whole album was written by someone called F-Daddy. And why should Kevin be surprised? When they were kids, everyone knew Smallie was dyslexic. He could barely read a few words without a tutor.

"That company," the mom said, "they even made my boy put a tattoo on his belly, some nonsense like 'Thugs Rule.' "

"Still, it's not the company that dissed the Bishop," said Kevin. "It's F-Daddy who wrote that deadly line, 'Mr. Shue, we'll nail your crew / a burning cross waits for you.' That's what killed Smallie. They just shot the wrong guy!"

But now Kevin had a chance to shoot the right one.

He hid well behind a fat lamppost, checking his flash one more time. He was in prime ambush position. He already had F-Daddy in his sights, from the back, while the dog relieved itself in a steady stream. The key was keeping his camera steady as he crept up on his prey. Kevin had even perfected his own technique. He held his breath, completely, and used his tight diaphragm to steady his upper body, his arms.

But then the whole world was spinning. That dog was so quiet Kevin didn't hear it come up on his ankle. But he felt its teeth sink into his skin. He tripped, landed well back on his butt. His extrabright flash, the one that stunned its victims, caught *him* in the face instead of F-Daddy.

He was now blind, his pupils shrunk, corneas quivering somewhere in his aching skull. But it wasn't spots that he was seeing; it was like this white sheet that grimaced. It was an angry, white-looking guy looking down at him, pulling him by the neck, smashing his camera onto the curb.

"Jesus," said Kevin, realizing his mistake. This was a big white guy too, well fit and muscled into his spandex, even though he looked around forty and bald. "I'm sorry, mister. It's a mistake, really. Forgive me. I'm out of here right now."

"What are you babbling about?" said the white guy. "You're a stupid shit, you know that?"

"No, I'm a magazine writer," said Kevin. "I fucked up, I mean, I think I was set up by those Universe guys. They said you were F-Daddy, this guy I'm looking for. But as I just said, I'm like . . . going."

"Now hold on," said the white guy. "You fucked with me, now you listen to me. I know about you."

"What?"

"I *am* F-Daddy, you dumb son of a bitch."

"But," said Kevin, "you're . . . You got a bald head. I mean, those security guys put you up to this. You guys are just bullshitting me to get some money."

"You are a pathetic asshole—"

"Hey, hey," said Kevin, who knew he looked like a lame-to-the-wood sissy boy, but still. "Be careful how you insult me. I may not look like much, but I could snap too, you know. I mean, how do I know you're for real?"

"And how do I know you're real?" he replied. "How do I know you don't have some homeboys hiding around the corner?"

"Well," said Kevin, "if I were going to fuck you up, would I be doing it with a thousand-dollar camera, which you smashed, thank you very much."

"Sorry," said the guy. "So you don't think I'm the notorious F-Daddy because I'm white?"

"Well . . ." said Kevin, being careful how he chose his words. He didn't want to make this guy crazy again. "You are old."

"You don't think my shit is real?"

"Well, I can't believe you wrote the rap that got Smallie killed."

"Well, nigga, why don't you test me? I'm down."

Kevin wasn't exactly sure what he meant by this. But he thought of something that could end all these people playing with his mind.

"Okay," said Kevin. "Can you translate this for me. It's from an F-Daddy CD." He thought a minute, and kept enough distance between him and this guy just in case he had to run for his life. "Ladies wee-wee when they peep me / Mohicans wax me in they wigwam."

"Shit," said the white guy. "That line is from my hit single, 'Sniper Bitch.' Translation? Women get hot when they see me and strangely when I visit Indian reservations these promiscuous ladies try to seduce me in their houses."

"Uh-huh," said Kevin. "One more test to be extra sure." This was all too much to believe. It was like this whole place, with its blank street signs and spaghetti doorbells and everything the same, it was all fucking with his head. "Translate this: Nigga, don't know what's holdin' ya / I'm checkin' ya / but once ya draw back them lips, let the chips begin."

"Damn," said the white guy. "That's from 'A Ho's-A-Ho-A-Ho.'

I'm impressed that you know it. Hardly anyone remembers that one. That's the old school. Now to put that into my peeps language: It says, I am trying to make some contact with you and as soon as you respond with a grin, I will make peace with you."

"F-Daddy?" said Kevin. "This is bad news."

"No, bad news is you. You sneak up on people and ruin their lives with all that gossip. But I didn't know Smallie, see. I'm just a writer. I got an agent, and he handles the sales. Half the time I lose track of who buys and sings my shit. I didn't plan on Smallie getting killed. It's just words I wrote."

"You have no idea. When people find out that a white guy like you made Smallie a star, his mom can forget about royalties to pay for her son's big funeral, his fans will go whoosh, make a sucking sound like an asshole blowing in instead of out. . . . Damn, why'd you even tell me? I was about to go."

"Well, I figured if a jerk like you could find me I couldn't hide forever. And how did you find me? This place is so new it's not even in the city plans yet."

"Your agent," said Kevin. "Because I'm such an asshole, as you say, I majored in computers in college. I can break into most systems. I can peel open an E-Mail box in eight seconds."

"So now you'll ruin Smallie's rep? Destroy his mom's retirement fund, and expose me? Man, you guys are the real assassins. That's why they call you the POP-erazzi. You get it, *pop*!"

"This is big," said Kevin. "I would've exposed you, but now that you broke my camera I don't have anything to show. And what about some justice for Smallie? You're the one that should've been shot."

"Nigga, you don't even know who my friends are," said F-Daddy. "Kill me, did you say?"

"See what I mean?" said Kevin. "Just listen to yourself. Nigga this, nigga that. Man, you go around with that, sooner or later someone's gonna put a serious cap in your ass. So why shouldn't I make a buck before you leave the planet? You hear what I'm saying? That word you use, that's like nitroglycerin. You roll that around your tongue, you keep doing the licky-lick with that, and *it will* explode in your mouth!"

F-Daddy picked up his too-quiet dog and cradled it in his arms like a newborn baby.

"What's your point?"

"Shit, man, look at Huckleberry Finn, that book about Nigger Jim. Some white guy wrote that over a hundred years ago, nearly every line going nigger, nigger. And you know what? Right now, today, you got white teachers getting fired for just reading those words they didn't even write. Hey, hey—"

Kevin was talking to the lamppost. He didn't finish his speech. F-Daddy had gone, but where? He just disappeared on the dark street with no signs and the houses all alike. Shit. Kevin knew he'd never find him again. He was back where he started, knowing there was no Universe Security for him. Those guys could've made this up, all of them, as one of their bets. Now all these assholes needed was a reason to stop him, to strip him, and to search him. In his own guide he found cases where white cops detained brothers just for wearing fat jewelry around their necks, cops saying that the gold was probable cause. Kevin took off his crucifix.

He knew that when blackness stretches itself across town, beyond the tracks, so to speak, it's always to serve—it's a sign of submission. He remembered that from somewhere.

Right! The bastards kept his camera. He paid them the two-fifty. The security guys laughed in his face, taking him to an ATM machine. They waved an undeveloped roll of film under his nose. "We snapped F-Daddy," they chanted like spoiled children. Luckily his editor offered $10,000 and they pounced on it. But when Kevin got into his rented Mercedes S-280, he jammed the gas, then flipped a finger out the window as the car squealed away.

"Assholes!"

With a scoop like this, he was staring at six figures, easy.

"So, is he a street renegade with a knack for coopting rap rhythms, or a morph who insults minorities? Let's take the next caller from Clifton, New Jersey. You're on the air."

All day long Kevin sat in his office listening to talk radio. F-Daddy was all over the dial. He'd made the headers in yellow and red:

WHITE LIES: F-DADDY KILLED SMALLIE

EVERYTHING IS ALL WHITE FOR THE RAP ELITE

"Word up, word up."

Suddenly dee-jays all over the country were reading CDs. Rap lyrics by F-Daddy were turning up everywhere, like on the labels of America's top rappers, the legends themselves who sold folks on the image that they were Straight Outta Compton. One producer with a new group that was gaining notoriety even broke into a record store to hide the truth from the group's newest fans, who thought that these guys were so raw, so street, they'd be bigger than the Wu-Tang.

Kevin's editor finally called the only bodyguards she'd trust given the widespread death threats scanned on Kevin's voice mail. She called the NAACP, since she knew their condemnation of gangsta rap. They said it defiled Black women, with all its booty calling on MTV.

Kevin couldn't resist listening to the radio. Brothers and sisters called him everything from a race traitor to a hero for finally helping Smallie's mom get justice. She herself was filing a big lawsuit against the record company as well as the real villain behind this senseless murder, F-Daddy, whose real name was Frankie Diello. The lawsuit also indicted the agent who sold F-Daddy songs to rappers by concealing his true identity.

Then on one show, Smallie's mom pleaded with angry fans not to waste their rage on Kevin. He was only the messenger. And, choking back tears, she quoted the now infamous words of Rodney King: " 'Can't we all just get along?' "

Kevin was grateful for the thought, but he was also realistic: Those hard-core rappers whose careers he ruined were not known for turning the other cheek. Even if they wanted to turn it, their fans expected them to respond like true gangstas. Long before Smallie, in fact, Kevin had written a caption beneath a photo of a rapper who'd been blown away in a drive-by: "Forget About Yo Money: Rap's problem is that there are too many feuding rap stars, managers, and deranged entourage members roaming the streets. Hip hop's #1 priority: Watch your back."

Kevin grabbed his cell phone—the only one at the magazine not flooded with irate callers. He dialed King Palace Motors. What could he buy for $140,000? That was nearly all he'd earned on the F-Daddy photos. The salesman's voice bubbled when he heard Kevin's name. Since the photos had appeared, he'd already sold two bulletproof cars right off the showroom floor to rap stars who themselves used F-Daddy songs and now feared the wrath of disappointed fans. For Kevin, the salesman had a special deal.

"But for God sakes, don't write about it."

For Kevin, he'd cancel a sale originally ordered by the security staff of the president of Guam. For $140,000, Kevin could get an Econoline van with reinforced windows and side armor capable of withstanding a direct hit from a rocket launcher.

"Your eardrums will bleed," said the salesman, "but you'll live."

The van also came with carbon plating that covered the vehicle's entire underbelly, including the engine, gas tank, and roof.

"And," said the salesman, "you get rubber-filled run-flat tires that can achieve seventy miles an hour after they've been shot out."

And if the going gets tough, the salesman explained, the van could even be customized with a pop-out roof so someone can stand up and blast from behind. Kevin made it clear that he'd have to run this expense by his editors since they had a hand in his trouble.

"Well then," said the salesman, "mention the Level-Three armoring. This van's equipped to shoot tear gas in all directions and it comes with a pain generator capable of broadcasting a sound so piercing anyone within fifty feet will drop to his knees and start vomiting."

Kevin's editors were suspiciously gone for the day. He'd have to pitch his expenses later. He now had to pee from all the coffee he drank trying to stay awake until he got home safe. He hadn't slept since meeting F-Daddy, a day ago.

Seeing the righteous brothers guarding the employee bathroom, Kevin's caffeine-wracked nerves were calmed. He washed a cold sweat from his brow and neck with a wet paper towel. Then he stood at the urinal with his dick in his hand, like all men in this stupid position, waiting to shake off, his eyes focused on the bathroom tiles.

"Fuck you, asshole."

The voice startled him. He had to stop peeing in a hurtful, liquid gasp.

"Damn, what are you doing here?"

Frankie Diello was on the fire escape outside the bathroom window.

"Making sure," said Frankie, "if my ass goes down because of what you did, your ass comes with me."

"Hey," said Kevin, "I already got rappers waiting to suck my blood through a straw. And I still have to finish my pee. So I don't need you, thanks."

"Look," said Frankie. "Believe me, those rappers are not your problem. Those suckers got something to live for. They're not going to kill you. They got bank accounts and contracts to worry about. Besides, my agent's already been on the horn with them. See, the fact is, rap's biggest audience is white and male, eighteen to thirty-four. And those *wiggers* are snapping up F-Daddy CDs because they know this shit's going to be a cult item. Sales are booming, homeboy. Besides, my agent already spoke to our company's Japanese backers and they're ready to sponsor a Smallie tribute with me and Smallie's mom, white rappers and Black rappers holding hands, swaying back and forth singing, 'We are the world' and shit. The fans will eat it up. It's the East Side Clan and Bishop Shue we got to worry about."

"What?"

"They want to kill me. I know that. But you, homeboy, it's all over the street. You exposed their mistake. They shot the wrong guy! You made the Clan look like assholes to the other crews, and now they gotta take you out, too."

Kevin's cold sweat was back. And he was still at the urinal, dick in hand, but now his urine tract must've acknowledged the threat. He tried, but nothing came out.

"So, why are you here? You taking me out first?"

"I should, after what you did. You see, you don't know where I'm coming from. You see, Kevin, where you come from, you're a college boy; when people like you have a problem with some organization, you have your lawyer contact their lawyer, right? But where I come from, it's white gangsta rules: If some group fucks with you, well, you have your thug contact their thug. Got it?"

"I got that."

Suddenly, someone was banging on the bathroom door.

"Shit," said Frankie, disappearing from the fire escape. "Follow me."

Kevin looked at the pounding door. He looked at the window. Then he zipped up so fast he caught his nuts in his pants. Wincing, he curled to the floor and yelped.

About the Author

These stories, in different ways, are mostly about the voices I grew up with in the South Bronx, the voices of both my friends and my enemies. They are as much about the guys who protected me as they are about those who beat me. They are the voices of Sucio, Pablo, Babalou, Alphabet, and Bleachy, as well as the Turbans, the Savage Skulls, the White Angels, the Golden Guineas, and many more. They are the voices of my past as well as the voices of my present. These stories include the voices of my students, those in my English classes at La Guardia Community College who now live in my old nabe, and live in places like Bed-Stuy, Hollis-Queens, and Harlem, who share their street stories with me. What's changed? Among my old friends, as many are dead from knives and guns as those who are killed on the mean streets of today. What's changed? The language, yes, the street slang, and the fact that thugs now sing about what they do. They get music videos—we didn't. What's the same, however, is the attitude, the gangsta mentality. That's forever, as far as I'm concerned:

Whether it's the 1920s Al Capone gang or the gangs of *West Side Story* or the L.A. Bloods, all of them, all of us, share the golden rule of the street, of drug addiction, of poverty, of child abuse, and of broken homes and dreams: DO UNTO HIM . . . BEFORE HE DOES IT TO YOU.

—Peter Rondinone

FAST-PACED, HEARTBREAKING, ALTERNATELY FUNNY AND FURIOUS, alive with new language in every sentence, *The Digital Hood* announces a new voice in American writing.

These stories portray young people in the South Bronx and Los Angeles who find coded ways to speak—digitally over the Net, graffiti-tagging on walls, overpasses, and billboards, or rapping. The language in this book is theirs, and each story in some way touches on the question of who controls speech, and what it means to be silenced.

The gang leader who narrates "Something for Sucio"; the girl with a crush on a graffiti-writer in "The Nobody"; the victim of police torture in "To Break a Nigga's Neck"; the risen-and-fallen rapper in "Gangsta Bond"; the bewildered elderly couple in the riot-torn L.A. of "You People"; the middle-class man who can't escape his past in "My Protector"; and the gleeful, imaginative hacker of "The Digital Hood"—their voices and stories are unforgettable.

Advance Praise for *THE DIGITAL HOOD*

"I read *The Digital Hood* right away and straight through. It is the real thing. There isn't a false moment. No question about it, Rondinone has a great ear for the language. I can't wait to read his next book." —CLARENCE MAJOR, author of *Dirty Bird Blues*

"There is a remarkable power in *The Digital Hood,* and that power comes from the writer's ability to allow the people of the street to reveal themselves to us. Reading this book is an exceptional experience." —HUBERT SELBY, Jr., author of *Last Exit to Brooklyn*

(continued on inside back cover)